Tales from The Foxes of Foxham

Matteo Sedazzari

Published by ZANI

Tales from The Foxes of Foxham © Words–2021 by Matteo Sedazzari. Electronic compilation/ paperback edition copyright © 2021 by Matteo Sedazzari. © Illustrations – Andy Catling

For information contact:
info@zani.co.uk

Front Cover and Inside Cover design by Andy Catling
https://www.catling-art.com/

Tales from The Foxes of Foxham is in loving memory and dedicated to my grandparents, Gladys and Ernest Vine, who introduced me to foxes and the wonders of Norfolk, and my Italian grandparents, Ines and Mario Sedazzari, who introduced me to Italy and the magic of that country.

A big thank you to everyone and anyone who bought and supported my first two novels, A Crafty Cigarette–Tales of a Teenage Mod and The Magnificent Six in Tales of Aggro, you have made a happy fella… thanks again x

Thanks also to those who supported me during the process of me writing Tales from The Foxes of Foxham, you know who are…..

And thank you to those of you who are holding a copy of this book. I hope you enjoy a classic tale of foxes, witches, bears and humans in the fight for good versus evil.

The Tales Trilogy from Matteo Sedazzari and ZANI

A Crafty Cigarette – **Tales** of a Teenage Mod
The Magnificent Six in **Tales** of Aggro
Tales from The Foxes of Foxham

When I began to write my debut novel A Crafty Cigarette – Tales of a Teenage Mod, my first point of research was my emotional recollection. As I started to recall personal experiences and feelings from my youth and childhood, I realised that popular (pop) culture plays an important part in our lives, not just in terms of entertainment but also personal development and growth, from a moving film to a powerful song, that can change your life forever.

For me, prior to donning a parka and learning all the lyrics to The Jam's songs, American crime films, classic children's literature, British comedies, holidays in Italy and Norfolk, and much more, had been and still are, instrumental in my progress.

Therefore, I wanted to include many pop cultures in my debut novel A Crafty Cigarette – Tales of a Teenage Mod, the traditional semi-autobiographical author's first book. Yet, as I started to write Crafty I found that the book was moving away from the facts, and into the whelms of fiction. Yes, the essence of being a Mod and a Jam fan are true and many of the key characters in the book are based on real people, yet many of the events are not, for instance my father never knew nor worked with Charlie Cairoli, nor did he have a hatred for clowns, and I never broke into my next-door neighbour's house.

When I finished writing Crafty, I was pleased that I had honoured Mod and The Jam. Moreover, I wanted to write another book, yet for my second one I wanted it to be a homage to the London based TV shows that I enjoyed, Only Fools and Horses, The Sweeney and Minder, comedy characters like Fletcher from Porridge and Private Walker from Dad's Army, the City of London itself, and the Casual movement of the early 80s.

I didn't want to restrict the story to one time frame and one sequence of events. Therefore, I created six key characters, a gang of Casuals, The Magnificent Six from White City, Shepherds Bush, who became the hub of the novel, and from them I could span different generations over different decades in an anthology.

Simply entitled Tales of Aggro, as a homage to the mentioned genres, a nod to Roald Dahl's Tales of the Unexpected and to create a theme, 'Tales', novels penned by me as a tribute to pop culture.

I later on retitled Tales of Aggro to The Magnificent Six in Tales of Aggro, with a new cover. I had started to work with illustrator Andy Catling on Tales from The Foxes of Foxham, and through his work I knew he could add magic to my second novel. From our brief discussions I thought changing the title would give the novel a new lease of life.

Tales from The Foxes of Foxham, the tributes are simple, classic children's novels that were important to my childhood, Wind in the Willows, 101 Dalmatians, The Lion, The Witch and The Wardrobe, Enid Blyton's The Faraway Tree, stories that transported me out of my bedroom to the land of adventures, with good folk fighting the bad folk. Holidays in Italy and walks in the woods of Norfolk with my grandparents, looking for red foxes…. Magic and… Love.

In short, my 'Tales trilogy' are tales of the imagination inspired by pop culture and the odd real event.

Happy reading

Matteo Sedazzari
Feb 2021
Tales from The Foxes of Foxham

Table of Content

1

When Winston met Charles...

October 1943—The jet-black Rolls-Royce Phantom III gleams under the bright full moon as it pulls into the long and winding gravel drive of the Elizabethan house, Fox Hill Hall, situated on top of a small hill in the village of Foxham in Norfolk and giving the suave and sophisticated 'Lord of the Manor', Charles Renard, a splendid view of his beloved village from his study. Yet Charles does not spend all his time watching over the community, for he is an extremely busy fox.

Hearing small stones being squeezed by the powerful tyres of the Rolls Royce, Charles leaves his cosy study to greet his guest. As he opens the study door, standing before him is his faithful and highly intelligent friend and butler, Boris Bates, a badger dressed in a black tailcoat jacket with a bright, white, immaculately ironed Windsor shirt.

For the first year of his service to Charles, Boris would wear dark grey wool trousers, yet he found every time he bent over, the trousers would split in the rear end due to his big backside, so Charles said it was fine for him not to wear trousers any more. However, Charles loves wearing trousers, especially plus fours, as he has a range of colours for all occasions. And for this evening, he is wearing bright burgundy plus fours to complement his black with a burgundy collar silk and satin smoking jacket, and a burgundy embroidered smoking cap with a gold tassel.

'Will Sir care to have a sandwich and a drink before your meeting with the Prime Minister?' Charles smiles at his close friend and replies, 'Thank you Boris, but alas no, I hear his chauffeur-driven motor car approaching. Even though I could ravish

a chicken sandwich and gulp a dandelion wine quicker than a rabbit running down a rabbit hole, the man may see crumbs on my chin with damp whiskers, prompting him to ask for refreshments. Boris, please under no circumstances are you to give the man any alcohol until our meeting is complete. Only then serve any liquor if our conversation has a satisfying conclusion for us, the animals.'

'Quite agree, Sir, it is funny that man now seeks the help of the animal, especially the fox.'

'The rich man, yes, but the poor man, most of the time has been kind to us. But the rich man likes to hunt us and give our furs to their wives,' says an angry Charles, with Boris nodding in full agreement.

'Sir, may I request that you and the Prime Minister do not speak too loud as your wife Kaye is nursing a cold,' states the ever-caring Boris. 'I will try my utmost to control my temper, but the Prime Minster does irritate me. And speaking of irritations, where is that rascal son of mine, Ferdy? I cannot have that muttonhead crashing through the doors, looking for an excuse for merriment.'

'Foxy has taken a break from his studies to take Ferdy for a drink down the Six Bells. I walked into the village this lunchtime and requested that the landlord, Horace, lifted Ferdy's lifetime ban for this evening only. I gave him a crown for his troubles.'

'Splendid work, Boris. Foxy is a good son and Horace is a hard-working and honest landlord who doesn't need Ferdy selling meat, clothes pegs or whatever to his thirsty customers. It breaks my heart to think that my son is a spiv, shaming the family name of Renard. Boris, I hear a car door opening. I am going into the drawing room. Please open the front door and show Mr Churchill to the drawing room.'

'Of course and good luck, Charles,' says the supportive Boris. Charles nods in appreciation.

■ ■ ■

Charles Renard was born 1904 in the then Stoke Ham Village, Norfolk, to Jacques and Lucetta Renard, two foxes, that in 1899, emigrated from the outskirts of Paris to England looking for farm work—as fox labour was, and still is, a new thing, because at the turn of 19th century (1801 in fact), foxes started to walk on two legs and speak like humans.

In fox folklore, many believe that the great fox, Jasper Ludham, of Ludham Village, Norfolk, was the first fox to speak and walk when being pursued by the aristocracy in a fox hunt. According to the legend, after bumping into an old woman in the woods, Jasper stood up on his hind legs, turned to the hounds and screamed out 'Tally Ho,' making the hounds flee in terror, whilst the horses bolted, throwing their riders into the air, with a few of the men breaking their necks as they landed, which was met by cheers from the nearby villagers, who loved the foxes.

The nearly 150-year history of the speaking fox is long and complex, with several contradictions. So, dear reader, I do not want you to fall asleep. However, it is fair to say, foxes in a short period of time, have come a long and remarkable way from being beautiful woodland animals.

Many humans across the world have embraced the new foxes, offering them work, and allowing them to settle. Still many, like the nobility, believe the only good fox is one that has been ripped apart by hounds or skinned, so their furs can be paraded in high society—resulting in some regions across the world allowing fox hunting and some not, such as Norfolk, where the first speaking fox was sighted, Jasper Ludham.

As the foxes developed across the world, they tried to pass on their knowledge to other woodland and forest animals, and even pets. Yet to date, only badgers, bears, wolves and some breeds of dogs can walk, talk and even think like humans. As these breeds of animals evolved in terms of intelligence, so did their posture, life expectancy and height. So, it is not uncommon to meet a four-to-five-foot fox or wolf, or dog or badger, aged 55 these days, standing on their hind legs.

■ ■ ■

At an early age, Charles showed a true aptitude for accounts, which allowed him to rise above being a farm paw, and doing the accounts for his parents' then employer, Lord of Stoke Ham, who resided in Stoke Ham Hall. Soon, word got out about the clever young fox and his natural ability with numbers. Therefore, many were offering him good money, from farmers to butchers, for his services. Soon, Lord of Stoke Ham appointed the young Charles to be the manager of their bank. Little did Lord of Stoke Ham know that Charles was secretly plotting his demise. Because back then, foxes were still crafty with rich humans, after years of brutality, and it was their cunningness that kept them alive for many centuries. Yet today the fox can still be crafty, so if you have foxes as neighbours, treat them with respect, otherwise they, too, could be plotting your downfall.

The bank flourished and so did Stoke Ham, as Charles helped the local businesses, and in turn more money was put into schooling, housing and general upkeep of the village.

Like all industries, the world of banking is small and Charles' achievements did not go unnoticed. So, it was no surprise that one day, Charles received a letter from the Bank of England requesting his services. Charles Renard was the first fox in the world to be offered a job in a big organisation.

After accepting the job offer, Charles rented a room in nearby Hackney, which boasted the largest fox population in London, who called themselves urban foxes and jovially frequented the music halls and the pubs. The various inhabitants of Hackney loved the foxes, as they added zest to their already vibrant community. Charles enjoyed Hackney. Yes, it was rough, but he treasured how different religions and races could live and work side by side. You will be pleased to know that the fox community is still thriving in this part of East London and beyond.

Sadly, at the Bank of England, Charles was often bullied for just being a fox. Colleagues would shout out, 'Tally Ho,' or come in wearing their wives' or girlfriends' fox fur and asking Charles if the fur was an aunt of his. Nevertheless, the strong-minded Charles showed these cruel men no tears—he simply ignored them and carried on with his work, as well as investing his money wisely. But when Charles returned to his bedsit, he would weep himself to sleep.

Then, one day, he punched one of the main tormentors, a rogue from Eton called Basil Rose. Charles hit him so hard that Basil lay on the floor unconscious for about five minutes. Charles was sacked on the spot but he didn't care—Charles had enough money to retire from banking and buy Stoke Ham Hall, as he knew, thanks to his parents' letters, that Lord of Stoke Ham was nearly penniless due to his love for wine, women and song. The man was down, and this fox was about to give him one almighty kick.

Lord of Stoke Ham, in desperation, sold his family home for a song, and left Norfolk to travel Italy in search for inspiration. The day after the sale, Charles renamed the house Fox Hill Hall, and the village from Stoke Ham to Foxham. Charles wanted this to be a fox community and a place of pilgrimage for foxes from across the world. Many humans remained in the newly named Foxham as they liked Charles more than the Lord. Moreover, Charles Renard is now the leader of foxes in Europe and that is why Winston Churchill has requested an emergency meeting with him, seeking the fox's help in defeating Hitler and the Nazis.

Foxes across Europe are not conscientious objectors, yet when the War was declared, Charles ordered no foxes to fight, as he knew that the gentry British generals of the Great War of 1914 to 1918 ordered foxes to be the first to go over the trenches, knowing that many would ultimately face death as they weren't armed, therefore leaving vixens and cubs without a husband and a father. Charles believed the act by the top military personnel was an excuse to senselessly cull foxes.

However, Charles allowed foxes to work in factories, hospitals and such like to help with the war effort, with some foxes even joining the Home Guard in Great Britain, for the British foxes, like the British people, feared Hitler and the Nazis.

The foxes not joining the British armed forces was, for a while, no hardship, as Winston Churchill and his coalition government could not see any benefit in having foxes on the front line as they believed the foxes would upset the morale of the soldiers, pilots and sailors, with their crafty ways.

But now Churchill is planning an invasion of France for next summer with the American general Dwight Eisenhower, which they believe will bring the war to an end, so every available man, and now fox, is needed. Yet Churchill loathes the fact that he must negotiate with a fox. Yet it was Eisenhower who made Churchill seek a meeting with Charles, after Eisenhower won the support of Charles' American counterpart, Chuck Snack, a fast-food entrepreneur and loud-mouthed fox.

Chuck owns a highly successful hot dog restaurant in Lakewood Boulevard, Florence Avenue, in Downey, California. Nearby, there are two brothers, Richard and

Maurice McDonald, who are getting a lot of recognition with their burger bar. But Chuck believes they are no threat and chuckles when his daughter, Felicity, says they could be a household name. 'Gee, no one is going to say, "Do you want a McDonald's?" They are going to say: "Let's have a Chuck's."'

■ ■ ■

Churchill takes one last puff on his cigar, as he waits for the chauffeur to get out and open the car door. The moment he steps out of the Rolls Royce, Boris opens the large oak Elizabethan door and starts to walk down the spectacular stone steps to greet the guest.

'Mr Prime Minister, Master Charles Renard waits for you in the drawing room. Will you please follow me?' says Boris, as orderly as ever.

Churchill is taken aback by how smart the badger looks in appearance and his manners are the best he has ever seen in a butler. 'Please call me Mr Churchill. And you are?'

'Thank you, Mr Churchill. I am Boris Bates, head butler of Fox Hill Hall.'

The walk from the Rolls Royce to the drawing room takes less than five minutes, and Churchill again is taken aback to see a splendid looking and well-dressed fox. Charles smiles, walks forward and holds his paw out with pride, and without any hesitation, Churchill shakes his paw, as he senses a worthy fox standing before him. However, Churchill wants to control the conversation, and does so, by saying: 'Does your son, Ferdy, do nylon stockings as I need some for my wife?' Churchill had sent Dalston and Towner of the Yard to watch Charles and his family a month ago, and they came back, saying they were far from Nazi sympathisers, but the son Ferdy was actively involved in the black market and asked if they could shoot him. Churchill pondered for a minute, before firmly saying: 'No.'

Charles is not fazed by Churchill's opening question, knowing that he would have done his research. 'My son, Ferdy, is a business fox, as he owns the local fish and chip shop, and I know from time to time, unsavoury characters enter his premises for cod and chips. Sometimes, they plead poverty and offer goods in return for food, so my son takes the goods and sells them in the village, donating most of the money to the church, like all good Christian foxes do. Yet when he returns from his Bible studies, I will ask him.'

'Bible studies my backside. Your son is a spiv.'

Charles, knowing that Churchill is trying to get the upper hand by denigrating his son, replies with ease: 'The pressure of the war and handling stolen goods is getting to my God-loving and law-abiding son, as it is with many in Great Britain. I am sure once Hitler is beaten, Ferdy will return to his former, kind ways. But, for now, I request you waive the persecution of my son, as we are here to talk about the war and how foxes can help.'

Churchill is impressed with Charles' strong and confident reply, as Churchill has seen and heard with his own eyes and ears that Charles is a born and powerful leader.

'That is correct, Charles. I am here to talk to you about the war. We need manpower—well, fox power,' says Churchill, hoping his closing words will amuse Charles.

Yet Charles gives Churchill a frosty stare, then says, 'We do support you, Mr Churchill, as every fox in Great Britain does not want live under a Nazi regime. In Germany, there are some foxes who have sided with Hitler, yet there are many who haven't. I got a letter from my French cousin, Marcel, who is doing his bit with the French Resistance.'

'A brave fox, ready to put their life before the liberty of France and the freedom of Europe,' roars a proud Churchill, much to the annoyance of Charles.

'Yes, he and his friends are brave, yet like the foxes in Great Britain, the rich of France hunt foxes with dogs in their picturesque countryside. Madames parade around Paris with the furs of young vixens around their necks. How would you ruddy like it if my wife was to walk in here, with the skin of your aunt around her neck for the sake of fashion?' yells a now annoyed Charles.

'I would ruddy shoot her and you on the spot,' screams Churchill, as he pictures the skin of an aunt around a vixen's neck.

'And that is how foxes feel. We have learnt to speak and act like humans for less than 200 years, yet the aristocracy still hates us. But we are just creatures of nature that have a fondness for chicken and chocolate cake, with the penchant to be crafty in order to survive. The torment the rich have given us is nothing short of cruelty—something that even Hitler would be proud of,' says Charles abruptly.

Churchill, listening intensely to Charles' concerns, slowly nods in agreement, and replies, 'I now feel your pain. I never ever felt it before, Charles. Now, I see why you are the leader of foxes.'

Charles smiles at Churchill, gratified. 'This evening, when I return to 10 Downing Street, I will write an emergency bill to be passed first thing tomorrow in the House of Lords, banning Fox hunting and the wearing of fox furs, and I will ask our allies' leaders to do the same. Charles, I am not a man who pleads or begs, but I ask you for the last time, lead the foxes to join us in this fight against Hitler and the Nazis.'

Churchill sits down, now tired and in need of an alcoholic beverage and a hot meal. However, Charles, now sensing he is in control, steps into the centre of the drawing room and says, 'We, the foxes, are willing to give our lives to our beloved country. I thank you for the ban and now I ask that foxes can buy homes, as after I bought this place, oddly enough, an emergency bill was passed banning foxes, dogs and badgers in Great Britain from owning their own property. Too many animals are poor due to the greed of landlords. One last thing, and this is final, we want the same wage as a human. You will have to change the employee wages act that states, *"Any employees with a tail and fur will slow any work down, therefore in the name of God, they will be paid the third of a working man."* This is balderdash and madness, in the name of God, how absurd Mr Churchill.'

Winston Churchill is pleased that no one else, especially his deputy Prime Minister, Clement Attlee, is here to hear a fox speak to him in such an aggressive and demanding fashion. But with empathy, he replies, 'I will telephone Herbert Morrison again when I return, and request with immediate effect that foxes, badgers and some breeds of dogs be entitled to home ownership, along with a proper living wage, in… the… name… of… God.'

Charles, feeling a sense of pride and triumph, declares, 'Thank you, Mr Churchill. I will speak to my animals, and we will march with man side by side in this fight against the evils of Nazi Germany. Now, would you join me for a late supper of roast chicken, roast potatoes, peas, followed by apple crumble, washed down by a few light ales in the dining room?'

Winston Churchill breathes a sigh of relief, as his cravings for food and drink were increasing by the second. 'Charles, it will be an honour to join you.' With that, Winston Churchill gets up to walk with his new friend towards the dining room, with both knowing that their unity could just stop the threat of Nazi Germany.

2

Oliver's Army

Oliver and Geoffrey Cambridge are two young chirpy foxes, who are both gainfully employed as librarians at Cambridge University library, as books are their world. Since they were cubs, both Oliver (never Ollie) and Geoffrey (never Geoff) would read alone or read out loud to each other, as they lost themselves in *The Adventures of Tom Sawyer, Treasure Island, The Man in the Iron Mask, The Three Musketeers,* Sherlock Holmes—in fact, any adventure or detective story that would take these loving brothers to a magical world packed with thrills and dangers. Oliver adored Sherlock Holmes so much that he started to wear a deerstalker hat at an early age, whilst Geoffrey would don a battered straw hat just like Tom Sawyer.

Both were strong and healthy, yet neither Oliver nor Geoffrey cared to partake in the energetic activities of their siblings. As their brothers loved to play hide and seek or hopscotch on a hot summer's day, Oliver and Geoffrey took pleasure in reading in the small village of Boxworth, near the town of Cambridge, which then had and still does have a growing fox community.

The young foxes' kind-hearted and hard-working parents—Irena, a bookkeeper, and George, a carpenter—loved all their children dearly and equally. Yet they were both worried about Oliver and Geoffrey being cast out by the fox community due to their self-imposed isolation in reading, as it is the nature of a young fox to love mischief and to be crafty in the village or woods.

Their father, George, yearned for the day that the local police dog, a German Shepherd sidekick called PC Brutus, would knock on their small but cosy cottage one day, clutching Oliver and Geoffrey by the scruffs of their necks, saying he had caught them apple scrumping—for to get into trouble with PC Brutus

was considered a badge of honour by the young folk of Boxworth, for this police German Shepherd dog had a fierce reputation, as did most of his breed.

For German Shepherds across Europe have found gainful employment in the police, yet none have risen above the rank of PC, as the powers that be believe it is not God's will that a German Shepherd could be a sergeant or more. But when war broke out, the German Shepherds born and raised in Great Britain distanced themselves from Germany and started to call themselves Alsatians, in honour of Alsace the German Shepherd from a small village in Alsace-Lorraine created by the Germans on the French Border in 1871.

Alsace became not only the first German Shepherd in the world to speak but also the first dog, due to his aggressive manner, fearless ways and robust demeanour, to be employed by the police in his village in Alsace-Lorraine—for the local police feared Alsace may be prone to a life of crime.

Alsace relished his new role, from keeping the peace to solving crimes, thanks to his amazing scent and his skill in interviewing suspects. The accused, guilty or not, that were interrogated by Alsace would always confess to a crime, due to his 'persuasive nature'. It was rumoured in the village and beyond, that a cross-examination with Alsace was like being questioned by the Devil himself.

Alsace was feared by the innocent, the guilty and his fellow policemen, making Alsace one happy German Shepherd. His pioneering ways and 100 per cent conviction rate made police forces across the world highly keen to employ German Shepherds, male or female. It soon became the norm for German Shepherds to become police dogs. Yet there were many that wanted to be builders, postmen, butchers or chefs, yet no establishment would employ them in these roles, even though they are intelligent, strong and hardworking dogs with exceptional culinary skills.

■ ■ ■

As Oliver, in his deerstalker hat, and Geoffrey, in his straw hat, matured into fine and law-abiding foxes, proud parents Irena and George became even prouder when Oliver and Geoffrey became the first foxes to ever be employed by Cambridge University.

Then, one Saturday morning, as the whole family were having their full English breakfast, Oliver, Geoffrey and their two brothers, Harold and Cropper, received call-up papers from the Home Office. It was a day they all dreaded but knew was coming, as the whole fox community in the world had been told of the meeting between Winston Churchill and Charles Renard, where their leader Charles had agreed to join the war effort and stop the threat of the Nazi party. Therefore, all male, young and able foxes were to be conscripted for military service.

George and Irena cried all that day and night.

■ ■ ■

Oliver, in his battered deerstalker, along with Harold and Cropper, enrolled with the British Army, whilst Geoffrey, still wearing his straw hat, enlisted with the RAF. Since the war had begun, Geoffrey had started to read books on aeronautics and in the evening made model aeroplanes that delighted all the cubs and children, even the adult foxes and humans of Boxworth.

Oliver, Harold and Cropper began training with the Royal Fox Artillery. The three brothers were nervous at first; then the bravery, dexterity and intelligence that most foxes possess shone through and, within a month, all three were accomplished soldiers, with Oliver emerging as the natural leader, not just with his brothers but with his fellow fox soldiers.

All the foxes looked dashing in their military tunics and shorts, with their bright orange and white-tipped tails protruding. Charles Renard had insisted that the foxes in the British armed forces could wear shorts and, with the wearing of caps optional, Churchill agreed with no argument. This delighted Oliver and Geoffrey no end, as they could wear their beloved deerstalker and straw hats respectively.

As the Cambridge brothers were fast accelerating in the army, Geoffrey had shown a natural ability to pilot a plane, as had many foxes in the Fox Squadron RAF. Foxes were initially going to be used as observers, wireless operators and air gunners on the RAF bombers, certainly not pilots or co-pilots. Yet as many foxes in the RAF had shown the aptitude and willingness to fly, Churchill ordered the quick manufacturing of 500 miniature Spitfires for the Fox Squadron RAF. The human pilots were first encouraging to the new fox pilots, but this was short-lived, as the fox pilots relished at any given opportunity to loop, spin and tailslide their Spitfires, which was the main cause of fisticuffs in the RAF mess between the human and fox pilots.

Some foxes were made to join the Royal Navy, as sailors. However, foxes are certainly not water-loving animals, and foxes in villages and towns across Great Britain can be heard screaming when it is their bath night. Yet the foxes that were enlisted with the Royal Navy soon learnt to love the sea and the camaraderie between them and the human sailors, especially in their cabins playing cards where the foxes always walked away with their pockets filled with coins.

Dear reader, please never play cards with a fox, you will never win.

■ ■ ■

Winston Churchill and Charles had formed a trusting and respecting bond; it was not loving, but close enough. Yet it was so close that Winston Churchill insisted that Charles sat in their meetings as they planned D-Day, known as Operation Overlord, much to the annoyance of King George VI, General Dwight D Eisenhower and General Bernard Montgomery at St Paul's School in Hammersmith Road, London.

It was lucky for these men—and the whole world, in fact—that Charles was present, otherwise Operation Overlord may not have happened.

Derek the deaf and dumb dachshund would come into a classroom at St Paul's, which was now an operations room planning the liberation of Europe, to serve tea and food throughout the day. As the humans believed Derek couldn't hear what they were saying, they talked regardless, as the dachshund poured the teas and carefully placed the food, from hot sausage rolls to sticky buns, on a plate with a pathetic smile on his face.

Charles, with his animal instinct and nose, noticed that Derek's ears would slightly prick up when Montgomery outlined a manoeuvre and penetrate sweat when Eisenhower told the team of a plan, resulting with Charles asking in German (before the war, Charles had visited Frankfurt on several occasions for banking matters when he worked for the Bank of England), 'Wie geht es deiner Mutter? (**translated:** 'How is your mother?').

And, without thinking, Derek replied, 'Gut, danke. Ihre Haufen werden besser' (**translated:** 'Good, thank you, her piles are getting better').

There was a loud gasp as Derek made a dash for the door, yet Charles, a lover and player of rugby, tackled the fleeing spying dachshund to the ground.

'Well done, old boy,' yelled Montgomery.

'Gee, you're a swell fox,' shouted out Eisenhower.

'Charles, how on Earth did you know his mother had piles?' queried Churchill, who spoke better German than Charles.

'Thank you, General Montgomery, General Eisenhower and Mr Churchill, I didn't, but most human beings and animals care about their mother, so I just took pot luck,' answered Charles, at which everyone in the room started to laugh, apart from Derek, who was slumped on the floor in tears.

Derek was shackled and taken to the Tower of London, but spared execution as Nazi Germany had captured Bill Bangs, a Beagle, and James Slough, a fox—both spies—so Churchill wanted to exchange them.

Back at Derek's lodgings in the annexe of St Paul's School, Charles and the others found written notes and a timeline explaining Operation Overlord, which Derek was meant to send the night before to Germany via a network starting in London. But Derek got rather merry at The Red Cow pub next door, therefore missing his rendezvous, and thanks to Charles' quick thinking, Operation Overlord had not been foiled.

■ ■ ■

Oliver, in his deerstalker, looks up to the skies on the Higgins boat, the landing craft, as it approaches the shores of Normandy, for Oliver yearns to see his beloved brother flying high as he leads the air fleet of the flying foxes, but today, alas, no. Then Oliver sadly sighs, as he longs to be standing next to Geoffrey at Cambridge Library, checking in and out books for the tutors and the students, as they engage in pleasant conversations, instead of going into battle. Oliver is scared that he might never see his brothers or any of his family or friends again, and scared that D-Day might fail, and Great Britain and her allies will be forced to surrender to the Nazis.

But Oliver knows he cannot show his fear, as he looks at his platoon, 34 young brave and strong foxes, including his brothers Harold and Cropper, ready to land on a beach where only a few years ago you would have heard laughter, not gunfire.

The boat's ramp smashes hard in the sea, with salty seawater splashing hard into the faces of Oliver and his friends. Oliver clutches his rifle, grits his teeth, then releases them, as he shouts out, 'Tally Ho,' the traditional huntsman's cry, now used by British foxes in warfare.

Leading his foxes into the water, they quickly wade onto the sand, amongst the gunfire. 'I fancy an ice cream,' jokes Archie from Bristol, the joker in Oliver's army. All the foxes including Oliver laugh, as they know humour may just help them to survive today, 6th June 1944.

Oliver and the foxes had been instructed by Montgomery and Eisenhower themselves to steer their landing craft to the right side of the Normandy beach and head to the village of Caen, with the mission to capture as many tanks as they could and to prevent as much mortar and cannon fire as possible, whilst the humans, the 3rd Division, landed more centrally on the beach. Due to foxes' height and natural ability to go on all four legs, even though most have walked on two for the last hundred years, the Germans will have trouble noticing the foxes crawling in the sand as they will be heavily distracted by the main invasion.

Bullets whizz past the fearless foxes as they wriggle through the sand dunes. 'Heads and tails down, foxes. I can see a beach grass-opening 20 feet ahead. Keep crawling, and by Jove, please don't look up,' orders Oliver, with his troops obeying every word of his command.

As Oliver forecast, soon they are able to hide in the beach grass as they lay in wait for a Nazi tank or a small platoon carrying a mortar.

As soon as Oliver and his platoon sip water from their military bottles, with a few tucking into their cold chicken sandwiches, their short and well-deserved break ends, as they hear a Renault R35 tank approaching.

As the tank chugs along, the driver and his mate are oblivious to the fact they are being watched by foxes from the British Army hiding in the beach grass. Suddenly, a hand grenade lobbed by Mortimer, a keen cricketer fox from Brighton, lands in their hatch, exploding upon impact, making both men scream as it does.

Nevertheless, the grenade only acts as a smoke bomb, as the factory in Portsmouth, where vixens and their cubs are making arms for the male foxes, has been running low on gunpowder. Therefore, Oliver's plan was for the men to escape from the tank, believing there would be more of an onslaught, only to find guns being pointed at them by foxes. Oliver's plan went accordingly, as the two Germans had no choice but to surrender to Oliver's army, much to their annoyance and embarrassment.

'Oh no, we can't say we were captured by foxes, we will never live this down,' whispers the driver—in German, of course, to his mate.

'No talking,' orders Cropper, who looks at his brother Oliver with confidence, who nods back with approval. The remaining foxes foolishly put their rifles down, as they want to eat their cold chicken sandwiches and pork pies, leaving Cropper and Oliver pointing their rifles, as Harold, who like his friends wants to eat his lunch, is left with the task of tying up the men.

Oliver, and all the foxes hear the loud rustle of grass. The greenery aggressively parts and out steps 50 Wehrmacht foxes, with all their Mauser rifles pointing at Oliver and his troops. One of the Wehrmacht's foxes puts his rifle down, steps forward, and says in English with a German accent: 'Foxes, resistance is futile. Today, many of you and humans will perish to our guns. Please raise your paws and release your prisoners—I promise your execution will be painless. First, I will shoot the fox who thinks he is Sherlock Holmes.'

The fox leader of the Wehrmacht turns to his troops and repeats what he said in German. The German foxes start to laugh. In fact, they laugh so much and loud that they fail to hear the sound of blades propelling and the revving of a small engine, but it's a sound that Oliver and his platoon know all too well—the miniature Spitfire.

'Duck!' orders Oliver. All the British foxes do, as the Spitfires let their 303 machine guns fire at the Wehrmacht foxes.

'Run,' shouts Oliver's German equivalent, as the Wehrmacht foxes ditch their rifles and uniforms.

Seeing the naked German foxes flee, the miniature Spitfires cease fire, leaving Oliver and his platoon to compose themselves, and take control of the situation. The flying foxes fly off to watch and save more of their own. As they do, Oliver knows that his beloved and loyal Geoffrey has just saved his life. But he has no time for sentiment—a battle is needed to be won today.

■ ■ ■

Sadly, Archie and Mortimer were killed in combat, and Cropper lost a leg. Geoffrey and his flying foxes had two planes go missing in action. Their courage will never be forgotten on the day as they, along with other animals and humans, pushed back an evil dictatorship from taking over the world.

■ ■ ■

8th May 1945: Oliver, Geoffrey, Harold and Cropper, on crutches, leave the jubilant celebrations in Trafalgar Square for some refreshments—mainly a cold beer and some food. Like all of Europe, this is a day that they longed to see.

Witnessing the Royal Family, Winston Churchill and Charles Renard wave and speak to men, women, children, babies, foxes, dogs, badgers, and the brave brown bears and wolves of Europe, who had travelled to London for this, was wonderful. Peace and equality at last. Sadly, it took a war for this to happen.

By foot—or paw, to be more precise—Oliver and his brothers stumble upon a small pub, The Crown & Sceptre in Fitzrovia, which before and during the war had a strict 'no animal' policy; now everyone is only too happy to let these four brothers join them for their VE celebrations. The four fox brothers hug, laugh, swap jokes and anecdotes, dance and sing with all the human patrons, led by Geoffrey in his pilot's uniform and straw hat as he stands on top of the upright piano, as he gets everyone to sing *Knees up Mother Brown*, *Roll Out the Barrel* and such like.

Oliver is certainly a happy and proud fox, but still a hungry one, as The Crown & Sceptre has run out of food. But the landlord tells Oliver of a pie shop around the corner, and that he is welcome to bring his pies and eat them here. Leaving his brothers to the merriment, Oliver embarks upon a short and happy walk to buy as many chicken & mushroom and beef pies as he can afford and carry.

As Oliver enters the pie shop, which to his surprise is empty, he sees a young beautiful vixen standing behind the counter. 'Gosh, you look a hungry fox. Would you like a pie?'

'Yes, please, and, would… you… hmmm… care… to… well…' The vixen playfully chuckles upon seeing the soldier fox lost for words, then Oliver musters up the courage, and asks, 'Join me and my brothers for a drink around the corner at The Crown & Sceptre?'

'That would be delightful, thank you. I am Victoria. I want to be a journalist one day—the first ever fox to be one.'

'I am Oliver. I am going to own a library one day, the first ever fox to own one.'

They both start to laugh, for Oliver knows peacetime is going to be a good time to be alive and have dreams.

3

Alberto and The Witches of Benevento

'That is one fine fat young fox. I can't wait to stuff him with walnuts from our tree and roast fatty alive for our Christmas supper,' cackles Diana, a white-robed, blonde and beautiful witch, to her fellow witches, Andriana, Benedetta, Caterina and Carlotta, collectively known as the Witches of Benevento, with Diana being their leader.

The mystic-looking Andriana, in a colourful embroidered skirt, blouse and headscarf, just like a fairground fortune teller, adds, 'Don't forget to slit the fat fox's throat before you roast the porky cub. We must drain his blood.'

'Andriana, you always spoil the moment. Of course, Diana won't forget,' snaps the raven-haired Benedetta, who has the same attire of a fairground fortune teller, too.

Since Andriana and Benedetta joined the coven on the same day, 31st October 1907, 50 years ago, the pair have been fiercely competitive, much to the annoyance of their peers.

'Will the two of you shut up? There is a fox to be eaten and a spell to be cast,' orders Caterina, the older witch, slightly overweight with rotting teeth, who wears nothing but black, along with a black scarf. Even though Caterina is not the leader, she is seen as the mother figure of the coven due to her age and wisdom, coupled with the fact her mother Monica was the leader of the original Witches of Benevento.

But Monica and her fellow witches were burnt at the stake in the village of nearby Sant'Agata de' Goti in 1837. Caterina fled along with the coven's familiar, Ettore the black cat, when their home, Castello e Torre di Montesarchio, was raided by the villagers—mainly humans, with a handful of newly evolved foxes, as both species united to fight the evil that was terrorising their region.

From afar, the young Caterina, along with Ettore, witnessed the execution of her mother and friends, and she swore that night, as the flames burnt into the sky, that the Witches of Benevento would return. Caterina met the young Diana many years later at Lake Como, travelling Italy as she looked to start a new and more ruthless coven.

Diana became stronger in the mindsets of the two friends, leading the quest to recruit more witches. The merciless duo and their black cat travelled up and down the Bel Paese for many years to enlist genuine witches, not pretenders. They discovered Andriana with a travelling fair, causing mayhem near Verona, in 1901. And a few years later, the three witches, along with Ettore, sprang Benedetta out of San Vittore Prison, Milan, where she was being held for a minor theft offence, for they knew Benedetta was a powerful witch.

Just after the war, Caterina and Ettore came out of hiding and returned to Castello e Torre di Montesarchio, near Benevento, after the original occupants mysteriously vanished in the middle of the night. Caterina, told the nearby village that she was recently widowed due to the war, and her three cousins, who had lost their husbands in the conflict, too, would be moving in. The following day, Diana, Andriana and Benedetta arrived. It didn't even occur to the locals that the next generation of the Witches of Benevento had returned, as they believed these four women, along with a black cat, were harmless and in mourning—leaving the fearsome foursome and the cat to work on their dastardly plan to take over the world. Yet Diana wanted one more witch to make them feel complete, and just two years ago, 1955, Carlotta joined the Witches of Benevento, when Diana was visiting Naples for the day.

In 1955, the world was rock 'n' roll crazy, as was the 19-year-old Carlotta, who loved nothing more than to play the latest record of Elvis Presley or Buddy Holly in the evening after joining the coven. Her love for loud music annoyed the other witches a lot, yet being a teenager, Carlotta wouldn't listen to her elders.

Now aged 21, Carlotta is having restless nights, as she keeps getting visions that Buddy Holly is in danger.

Unlike the other witches of the coven, who dress in a more traditional fashion, Carlotta prefers to wear pedal pushers along with cropped shirts and brightly coloured flat shoes. A natural brunette, Carlotta has dyed her hair blonde, as she idolises Marilyn Monroe—in fact, she could even pass off as Marilyn's twin sister.

However, Carlotta is yet to give her soul to the dark side of the new Witches of Benevento, but Diana is confident she will do, as she, too, was once more concerned about her looks than sacrificing a poor innocent animal in order to cast a wicked spell. Besides, once a witch crosses over to the dark side, they can live for at least 300 years—well, as long as they aren't burnt at the stake, thrown in the sea or such like.

■ ■ ■

As for the animal that the witches intend to sacrifice for Christmas Day, which is tomorrow, it is a fat but happy and kind fox, Alberto Bandito, imprisoned in a large steel birdcage that hangs over a cauldron of boiling water in the upper kitchen of Castello e Torre di Montesarchio.

Alberto's father is a Neapolitan crime boss, Mario Bandito, a fox that is feared and respected across the whole of Naples and beyond. Mario was born into a life of crime, as his father, Lorenzo Bandito, was the best pickpocket fox in the whole of Naples, and took pride in teaching Mario how to pick a pocket or two. Mario soon mastered the noble art, as well as car and bike theft, along with shoplifting. But Mario and his friends never stole from the local shops or from their neighbours, only tourists and wealthy premises. Mario believed he was like Robin Hood, stealing from the rich and giving to the poor, but he always forgot the latter and just gave to himself.

Mario enjoyed the life of a petty criminal and it was only when he was sent to prison for a third time for bike theft that he wanted to become a full-time criminal.

Even though Mario was still a juvenile fox, Judge Azeglio Vicini believed that the scallywag Mario enjoyed imprisonment at the Naples Young Offenders home. Judge Vicini was right, as it gave Mario a chance to catch up with his friends, play cards in their dorms, football in the yard and pool in the common room, and cook home-made food in the kitchen as they planned their next little job.

So, Judge Vicini sent the young Mario to Casa Circondariale di Napoli-Poggioreale—considered the worst prison in Italy, as it is full of hardened men, foxes, dogs, wolves and bears. But Mario didn't fear doing his sentence, as his father Lorenzo had a few friends there, one being a human called Vittorio Mosele, a local mafia boss who respected and liked Lorenzo.

Mosele arranged it so Mario could stay in his large cell, along with his crew, where there was no curfew in terms of having the cell lights turned off. Mosele and his crew, mainly men and foxes, cooked their own food, drunk wine, played cards and sang songs, with the prison guards always joining in. Mario quickly went from being an errand fox to fully-fledged member of Mosele's gang and was offered employment with them when Mario was released from prison.

Mario only received 12 months for bike theft, whilst Mosele was coming to the end of a two-year sentence for counterfeiting extra virgin Bertolli olive oil.

Mario loved being a gangster, especially the tailor-made suits and silk shirts, and the respect he had from his parents, his peers and his neighbourhood, yet he believed he was not being fairly paid by Mosele, even though Mario had shown his worth by being a good enforcer and coming up with money-making schemes. But Mario was still living with his parents and had to ride a bicycle from Quartieri

Spagnoli to Mosele's sea-facing apartment in Viale Anton Dohrn, Chiaia, the upmarket part of Naples. For Mario, something had to give.

Mario knew Mosele was a keen fisherman, so one Saturday morning he suggested that they go fishing in the Bay of Naples. Mosele loved the idea, but Mario, like a lot of foxes, feared the water. However, Mario saw this as a good opportunity to talk things over with his boss alone, away from the rest of the crew.

Vittorio Mosele was never seen again. Mario said Mosele fell overboard, and the current took him away. In private, no one believed him, but in public, they believed his version of events. Mario declared himself leader and moved into Mosele's apartment, where he still lives today. Mario was no fool, so he paid his new crew a bigger cut, but he needed a right-hand man or fox, and in Mario's case, it came in the form of a Doberman, Diabolo.

Just before meeting Diabolo, Mario had met and fallen in love with Silvia, a fierce and strong-minded vixen, who owned Antica Trattoria e Pizzeria da Donato restaurant. For it was in this eatery that they met for the first time. Mario was complaining about the food; Silvia, who was in the kitchen at the time, heard a mob boss shouting at her staff, so she came out and hit him on the head with her saucepan. It was love at first hit.

On one of their first dates, Mario and Silvia were going for a leisurely stroll after lunch in the bay of Naples, where on the beach they saw a washed-up half-dead, liver-coloured Doberman. Both Mario and Silvia rushed to his aid, and Mario carried the half-drowned dog back to his apartment.

■ ■ ■

The Doberman was Diabolo from the streets of Tirana, Albania. A tough dog from a tough family, he wanted to travel the world, so after the Second World War he joined *Viaqua*, a fishing trawler, as a deckhand, to follow his dream and enjoy the Mediterranean Sea.

Unfortunately for him and the other animals on board—two wolves, Wilfred and Winston, a bear, Rocco, and one fox, Rossi, who unlike most foxes, had no fear of water—were treated appallingly by the three humans: the captain, Izet, Koll and his one-eyed brother Krojan. Diabolo and his newfound friends were forced to sleep on the ship's deck, and given cold gruel for breakfast, lunch and supper, whilst Izet and his chums slept in a nice cosy cabin and ate fine fish that they had caught in the day.

One night, when Wilfred, Winston, Rocco and Rossi were huddled up together to keep themselves warm, Diabolo decided to go into the kitchen and cook his best buddies some nice mackerel, along with some sauté potatoes. No sooner had the fish hit the frying pan than Krojan ran into the kitchen with a sword. Diabolo made a dash for it, shouting his pals' names as he did, but sadly for Diabolo, he slipped as he went onto the deck and fell into the cold dark sea, making a large and loud splash.

Rocco, the natural leader of the animals, saw his beloved friend fall to what he thought was his certain death and screamed out, 'Mutiny'. The other animals knew it was a call to arms. The revolt lasted less than 30 minutes, as Izet and his crew were blind drunk, and were no match for four strong brave and fearless animals. Fortuitously for the humans, their lives were spared. Rocco became the captain, but sadly he and his friends were unable to save Diabolo, who spent a week in the sea, unconscious.

Fortune smiled upon this poor dog, floating on his back as the waves carried him into the bay of Naples—in another hour or so, Diabolo would have been no more. Mario and Silvia nursed Diabolo back to life, both feeling an immediate affection towards this Doberman. Moreover, when Diabolo came round and got his strength back, he felt a warmth towards them, too, like he had known them all his life.

Mario asked him if he wanted to work in Silvia's restaurant or join him. Diabolo chose Mario and soon was a name in the underworld of Naples, due to his fearless ways and powerful presence. Mario knew that Diabolo would always be by his side.

Soon Mario and Silvia were married, with Diabolo as best dog. His speech had the whole reception in tears and he stole the show with his dancing after dinner. Mario was happy and now he wanted a bigger family.

On 1st October 1947, Alberto Ernesto Bandito was born. Mario was delighted to have a son, as was Silvia. As for Diabolo, he regarded Alberto as his younger brother. Alberto was born into love, protection, food and, of course, crime.

Yet Alberto wasn't interested in enforcing or stealing. Instead, he liked to draw, as he had, and still does have, a natural talent, and his parents and Diabolo are happy that he is happy, as Alberto wants to be a famous painter—the first fox to be one. Yet there is one thing that his family don't like: Alberto's love of food, from pasta to ice cream. It makes Alberto very overweight, yet he isn't a target for bullies, not just because of his father and Diabolo, but because he knows how to box, as Diabolo taught him at an early age. Besides, Alberto is a jolly and kind soul, always laughing and joking, and it was his laugh that got him the wrong attention—that of Caterina and Carlotta, the Witches of Benevento.

Caterina and Carlotta were at Naples market by the bay one Saturday morning. Caterina was there buying candles that had been imported from Haiti, and herbs that were unavailable in Benevento, whilst Carlotta was there to buy some rock 'n' roll records and new clothes. Caterina had wanted them to fly to Naples on their broomsticks, yet Diana had not lifted the broom flying ban. Besides, Naples, like all of Italy, fears witches, but thinks they have all been executed. Diana wants the people of Italy to believe this, until the day when the witches and their wicked friends are ready to resurface and conquer the world.

So, instead, Caterina rode pillion on Carlotta's black and white Lambretta Innocenti 150 LD, much to Caterina's dismay. Carlotta had seen not just the youngsters, but families bombing around on their scooters. So, like the first time

Carlotta heard Elvis, the first time she saw a Lambretta, she fell in love with the notion. Carlotta is very passionate about life.

As Caterina and Carlotta were walking through the market, they heard a loud laugh. They both turned around to see Alberto joking with the fishmonger. 'He's perfect for our sacrifice, to fulfil our prophecy,' whispers Caterina to Carlotta.

'I think he's cute,' Carlotta whispers back.

'Shut up. You know that if we drain his blood on Christmas Day and eat his flesh, we can cast the "i sogni dei bambini" spell—the curse that will send all the young to sleep and to have nightmares until the day they die, and then we can take over the world. Come on let's grab that fat fox and take him home.'

'Caterina, it is October. We would have to imprison him for two months. I am sure, by then, either the police or the mafia would find him. Look at him—he is the son of a crime lord. Can't you sense it?'

'For someone so young and foolish, you do speak wise words. I will send Ettore, our black cat, to follow and feed him—the fatter the better. Ettore can live by his wits and by the street for a few months. Now, let's fly back to Benevento and tell Diana of our cunning plan.'

Carlotta laughs and says, 'We came by scooter. Our brooms are still in the tower. When was the last time you flew a broom?'

'After the first war. And you?'

'I haven't. Not sure if I could yet. Anyway, I am the younger generation remember?'

That evening back at Castello e Torre di Montesarchio, all the witches laughed a wicked laugh—well, apart from Carlotta, but she hid her concern well. As for Ettore, their familiar, he was annoyed he was to spend the next two months following a fat fox, and when he found out he had a Doberman as a bodyguard, Ettore fainted on the spot.

■ ■ ■

Within a week of his mission to Naples, Ettore had won the trust of Alberto by turning up at his window, when the rest of his family were either asleep or out. 'Evening, Alberto. It is I, Ettore, your best friend with food, as I don't want you to die of hunger. You must eat, Alberto. Eat and eat.' Alberto didn't need any encouragement from Ettore, as food is as much his passion as drawing is.

Yet his love for fine or even basic Italian cuisine is putting a strain on the Bandito household. Mario, Silvia and Diabolo don't want to be cruel to the youngest member of the house—in fact, they love him dearly, and want the best for the young and cheeky Alberto. However, after their late-night supper, Silvia locks up the kitchen, just to prevent her son from eating food that is meant for a meal the following day. So instead, out of love, she puts a few biscuits in his bedroom, just to keep him going until breakfast.

Alberto is not a hermit fox. In the summer, he loves playing football in the streets of Naples with his friends—with Diabolo keeping watch, not just to protect his adopted brother but to make sure Alberto doesn't sneak off for a slice of pizza. And in the winter, Alberto either chats to his mother in the sitting room, as Mario and Diabolo are usually out 'on business', or draws in his bedroom. For the winter of 1957, it is the latter, as he knows Ettore will turn up with treats, from rice balls to beef lasagne.

Then on the night before Christmas Eve, Ettore asks, 'Would you like to come with me to "la terra delle torte e della pizza" (the land of cakes and pizza). It is nearby and the only time we can go is tonight. Would you like that Alberto?'

'Yes, please,' replies the impressionable young fox.

'Then come with me, young Alberto, come with me.'

Alberto, smiling and excited, climbs out of his bedroom window, yet the delight soon turns to terror as he is grabbed by Andriana, Benedetta and Caterina, who are hovering above his window on their broomsticks.

Diana had said, 'It is time that Naples knew that the Witches of Benevento are back,' much to the delight of Andriana, Benedetta and Caterina. Diana had remained at Castello e Torre di Montesarchio, along with Carlotta, who deep down does not like the idea of kidnapping an innocent young fox before Christmas. Yet she had told her fellow witches that she was going to get everything ready for the sacrifice.

Andriana throws the fighting fox into a brown sack, which Benedetta grabs, as she and the others, following her, fly off on their broomsticks towards the moonlight, cackling.

The sight and sound of these fiendish creatures of the night flying over the beautiful city of Naples scares the good citizens. Some fire shots from their guns, but many scream out, 'The witches are back.'

The loud uproar outside alerts Silvia, as she is reading a book in the sitting room. Her mother's intuition tells her that Alberto is in danger. Silvia runs into Alberto's room, only to see her son gone. Silvia falls to her knees and starts to cry…

4

The Terror of the Witches of Benevento

The petrified Alberto clutches onto the cold steel of the large metal birdcage that hangs above the witches' cauldron in the tower of the Castello e Torre di Montesarchio, which serves as the kitchen to this coven. As bellowing green steam rises to Alberto's cute and furry face, his fear is heightened as he observes animal skulls placed as ornaments alongside old leather-bound books on a dark oak kitchen cabinet opposite the black cauldron.

Across the wooden beams above Alberto's head hang many green yet dry herbs that smell bitter, unlike in his mother's kitchen where her herbs have an appetising fragrance. The countless large candles scattered around the kitchen flicker brightly, as the flames sway like they are caught in a mild wind. As Alberto observes the flickering light, he starts to shed a tear, believing this is the last thing he will ever see in his short time upon this Earth.

'Look, fatty is crying,' observes the wicked Andriana, which makes all the other witches cackle, apart from Carlotta, who turns her back to the coven and the captured fox. Then Carlotta turns around and looks at the other witches, who are too engrossed in their wicked laughter. Realising that only Alberto is looking at her, she quickly smiles in his direction, then turns away from him.

Alberto, the streetwise young fox that he is, knows it will be foolish to return the smile, as the witches will sense something is wrong. Yet he knows it is a smile of love that Carlotta has just given Alberto, the one thing he needs to survive this horrendous ordeal—hope.

Alberto, since his days as a young cub, had heard about the legend of the Witches of Benevento and how, one day, Caterina will return to the region of Campania to

cause havoc in revenge for the execution of her mother, Monica. But up until this very evening, Alberto had just thought they were nothing more than a myth from the region. When Alberto heard a Neapolitan talk about the return of the witches, the fox would just smile and nod, as all Alberto dreamt about was becoming the first fox to play and captain for Napoli and Italy, winning Serie A and the World Cup respectively, and for his paintings to be the main attraction at the Uffizi Gallery, Florence, earning Alberto millions of liras, so he can buy the best pizzeria in Naples, where he will eat pizza for breakfast, lunch and dinner.

As Alberto reflects upon the scary situation he is in, a voice inside his head says, 'Alberto, do not give up on your dreams, you can outwit these witches. You are a cunning and brave young fox, you are a Bandito.' The voice makes Alberto look up, and as he does, he catches the eye of Carlotta, who is standing behind the rest of the witches. She nods her head with a sense of approval. Alberto does not nod back, but he now knows he must act quickly to save himself, and unknown to him yet, the world.

'As I am to be sacrificed by you glorious witches, please let me know one thing: why? That is all I ask, and please call me by my name—Alberto,' requests Alberto in a humble manner.

'Very well, Alberto, as you wish,' declares the leader, Diana, in a defiant manner. 'We enchantresses—what the silly folk of Campania call witches—are like the foxes. We, too, are creatures of nature and the moonlight—it gives us our power and, from this, we can cast spells and perform magic. Many centuries ago, just as man was starting to walk the earth, our ancestors asked the foxes to join us, but the foxes said no, that their souls belonged to the light and our souls belonged to the darkness. That day was the day, we…'

'Witches,' says Alberto, as being cheeky is his second nature.

'Don't be an insubordinate fat fox,' roars a furious Caterina.

'Caterina, please be quiet. Alberto doesn't have long on this Earth. He is being disrespectful because he is nervous, as he knows he will soon be sacrificed,' replies Diana in a rare moment of consideration.

Then she continues her story. 'Alberto, that was the day we cursed the fox to stay a creature of the wood and to be hunted by man. We made man hunt, kill and skin you, hoping in time that all foxes will be extinct, like the dodo. Dodos had magic and light in their souls, so we convinced Dutch sailors to kill them all.' Diana, starts to cackle, setting off the rest of the coven, including Carlotta, but Alberto knows she is doing it not to blow her cover.

Alberto, now sitting cross-legged in the birdcage, as he is genuinely engrossed by what Diana is telling him, says, 'Please, carry on.'

'Little did we figure that the fox would become crafty and learn how to survive the fox hunt.'

'The fox hunt that was a cruel act of the rich man,' snaps Alberto.

'No, Alberto, the hunts were led by enchantresses and warlocks, men and women with noble titles that controlled the countryside, so the peasants of that land would allow their masters to cull the foxes in the name of tradition and honour.

'But our plan to kill all foxes was broken by the powerful wizard fox Jasper Ludham. How he became a wizard is beyond me, yet it is rumoured that a traitor of a witch gave him magic in his soul. Once he started to talk and act like man, he won the admiration of the pathetic ordinary folk, and soon fox hunting was perceived as a cruel act, but it was a great act.

'So now that foxes, bears, wolves and a few breeds of dogs walk and talk like man, it has weakened our power, which weakens by the day. What do we enchantresses get? Dumb yet obedient cats,' roars Diana, as she points to a rather petrified Ettore, before carrying on with her declaration. 'Yet our prophecy predicts that we will regain all our power by finding the fattest ever fox; then, we must cook him alive, drink his blood at the stroke of midnight on Christmas Day, and then we can cast "i sogni dei bambini".'

Alberto gulps, and with fear asks, 'What is "i sogni dei bambini"?'

'So pleased you asked Alberto, for it is a spell that will send all the young children, foxes, bears, wolves and dogs to sleep, where they dream a non-stop nightmare until they die. And when the young die, there will be no more humans, foxes, bears, wolves and dogs on this Earth. And we will become the rulers, with the ghouls, goblins and other creatures of the night as our citizens. Yet we will keep some humans and other animals alive to be our slaves. Just think, Alberto— your flesh and blood are the baptism to this new darker world.'

Alberto, now filled with anger, not fear, yet being the crafty fox that he is, doesn't show his true emotions. Instead, he pretends to weep.

'Look, he is crying again,' chuckles Benedetta.

'It is a shame you can't drink to celebrate this dawning of a new era,' sobs Alberto.

'Why can't we drink? We will if we want to,' snaps Diana.

Alberto smiles to himself, knowing he has got their leader's attention. 'Well, in the bars in Naples, the folk often joke if someone is drunk after one beer or a glass of wine, then they are a witch, because, in folklore, it says witches can't hold their drink.'

'They say what? Of course we can hold our drink!' screams an irate Andriana.

'Well, if you say so, but I don't believe you. My father told me at an early age that the drunk woman who you see staggering in the street is a witch or an ancestor of a witch,' says a now confident Alberto.

'Silence, nasty fox. Carlotta, go to the cellar and bring the wine up here. We will show this stout fox that we can drink,' orders Diana.

'Yes, Diana. How much shall I bring up? One or two bottles?'

'All of it. Yes, all of it. And get Ettore to give you a hand. We will have a party,' commands the leader of the Witches of Benevento.

■ ■ ■

Within an hour, Diana, Andriana, Benedetta, Caterina and Ettore the cat are on the floor, passed out after drinking no more than three glasses of red wine, as the rumour of witches being unable to hold their drink is proven to be true.

The tittle-tattle of witches getting easily drunk comes from the legend that one evening, Caterina's mother Monica and the other witches of Benevento got drunk after one glass of wine and boasted about being witches at a small inn in Sant'Agata de' Goti. This led to their arrest, trial and execution. As this small village was brave enough to see off the dark forces, it is blessed that no witch or their allies can set foot in this beautiful settlement without meeting their demise.

Carlotta, who can handle her drink, yet paced herself as she moved on from one glass of wine to a few cherry sodas, is standing stone-cold sober.

Suddenly, Carlotta rushes over to the birdcage. She unlocks and opens the door of the cage. The young, brave and clever but overweight Alberto leaps out, just missing the cauldron as he lands on his hindlegs.

'Come, Alberto, we must flee. One or two will wake from their drunken slumber, then they will see that we have vanished and give chase.' With this, Carlotta holds out her hand, and the happy Alberto puts his paw into her soft hand.

'Will we escape on your broomstick?'

'No, we can't. Ha, I have not mastered it yet, but I am an excellent scooter rider. Come on, no time to waste.'

With hope restored in Alberto's heart, he clutches Carlotta's hand, as she leads them out of the kitchen and towards the main entrance of Castello e Torre di Montesarchio.

Nevertheless, their bid for freedom is quickly cut short, when both he and Carlotta hear a familiar voice—that of Ettore, the evil black cat. 'Not so fast... hic. Fatty and you, Carlotta, will be banished to the abyss, to wander eternally as a... hic... lost soul. You betrayed us.'

Alberto, the kind but fighting fox from the streets of Naples, as Diabolo has taught his adopted brother well, turns to face the troublesome witch's familiar. 'I thought you were my friend,' Alberto says. Yet he is not asking for reassurance, just doing enough to confuse Ettore and stop him from raising the alarm.

'Your friend? Who could be a friend with a fat idiot like…' Ettore doesn't get to finish his sentence, as Alberto punches the nasty cat with all his might, just like last year's heavyweight boxing champion Rocky Marciano. Even though Rocky was born in America, Alberto's mother Silvia knows his mother, as she came from San Bartolomeo in Galdo near Naples and Benevento. In fact, they are good pen pals to this day.

'Bravo, Alberto. Now we must flee—the witches are starting to murmur,' says Carlotta, picking up Alberto so they can get to the entrance before the coven fully wake up from their drunken stupor.

Flying down the stairs of the castle, knowing that their lives and the world are in danger, Alberto and Carlotta get to the main entrance at such speed that even Jesse Owens would be impressed.

Alberto and Carlotta prise open the strong wooden door reinforced with steel. But freedom is one step away, as before them stands the bronze portcullis. Nonetheless, driven by determination, the fox and the kind witch pull down the chains of the heavy closed gate with strength neither of them knew they were capable of.

Alberto and Carlotta step out into the moonlight, as the beams shine brightly on Carlotta's black and white Lambretta Innocenti 150 LD. 'Wow, that is a beautiful scooter, but it should be light blue like Napoli, not the colours of Juventus,' says Alberto, as he spits onto the ground in disgust of his bitter football rivals.

'Alberto, shut up. Anyway, I support Juventus,' says a proud Carlotta. Alberto starts to walk back to the castle. 'Where are you going?'

'I can't get on a scooter with a Juventus fan—my father and Diablo will disown me.'

Carlotta sharply retorts, 'If you don't, you won't see your family again—or the world come to that. So now, just for tonight, be a friend with a Juventus supporter.'

Knowing that Carlotta is right, Alberto runs towards the Lambretta and jumps onto the back seat, as Carlotta takes her place on the front of the scooter. 'Alberto, if I kick-start the scooter, it will wake the witches. So, I will roll it down to the bottom of the hill. Hang onto me—it's going to be fun, my foxy friend.'

■ ■ ■

'Wee!' squawks Alberto, which amuses Carlotta, as she rolls the scooter down to the bottom of the hill of Castello e Torre di Montesarchio. Then Carlotta abruptly jolts the brakes as two smartly dressed wolves in three-button suits on light blue Vespas VNB1, followed by two white Fiat 500 Topolinos and a silver Alfa Romeo 1900 SS Cabriolet, approach them.

'Father!' yells Alberto.

'Don Mario Bandito,' whispers Carlotta to herself.

The wolves on the Vespas speed up, then brake to block Carlotta's Lambretta from moving, even though she and Alberto are stationary. All three cars skid and brake, the doors fly open, and a small legion of foxes, humans and one Doberman leap out, some bearing small pistols, whilst a few are carrying rifles.

Alberto leaps off Carlotta's Lambretta, holds his paws up and shouts, 'Father, Diablo,' as he runs towards them. Mario and Diablo put down their guns and smile, whilst Mario opens his body up to embrace the return of his kidnapped son. His men and foxes point their guns at the unarmed Carlotta, who has two snarling wolves on Vespas scrutinising her, with one of the wolves asking, 'Do you support Juventus?', which makes Carlotta chuckle.

'No, don't shoot her. She is my friend, Carlotta, she helped me escape. She, too, is fleeing from the witches. Don't shoot her, no,' pleads Alberto, as he breaks away from Mario's embrace to stand by the side of the fox Don.

'Men, foxes, put down your guns. Leonardo, Francesco—at ease,' orders Mario and they all obey. The two wolves pull their Vespas back from blocking Carlotta's Lambretta, as they turn their snarls into smiles, knowing now that the Marilyn Monroe lookalike is an ally who saved Alberto, the future Don.

'How did you find me so quickly?' asks a joyful yet tearful Alberto.

'Once the word was out that you had been kidnapped by witches, all of Naples and her surroundings came to our aid,' says an honoured Diabolo.

'Yes, we were told that the witches reside there, pretending to be widows due to the war, by these two wolves from Benevento,' says Mario, as he points towards Castello e Torre di Montesarchio with anger.

'Let's burn the castle down with witches in it,' roars one of the smartly dressed wolves on a Vespa.

'No... Leonardo...,' says Carlotta.

'How did you know my name?' asks Leonardo.

'Well, a lucky guess. Mario called you both by your names, Leonardo and Francesco, so I had a 50/50 chance of getting it right,' replies Carlotta in a rather sardonic manner.

Both the wolves, Mario, Diabolo, Alberto and the rest of the band start to laugh. 'I must say, Leonardo and Francesco, I like your suits,' remarks Alberto.

'Thank you, Signore Alberto,' replies a proud Leonardo.

'And I love your scooters. And the colour—do you support Napoli?' asks the ever-inquisitive Alberto.

'Yes, Signore Alberto. We are brothers that will support Napoli forever,' says a proud Francesco.

'Carlotta supports Juventus,' says Alberto without any malice. Yet the moment Mario's troops hear the word of their foe in football, all of them, apart from Mario, draw their guns and point them at Carlotta.

'No,' screams Alberto, as he runs in front of Carlotta holding his paws up.

Carlotta unfazed looks at Mario and his gang, and says, 'Shoot me if you like for supporting a different team, or listen to me and I will tell you how we can beat these witches. But it won't be easy. It's your choice.'

With such a confident statement from Carlotta, Mario's gang put down their guns, knowing how foolish they have been.

'Thank you. So, as I was saying, Leonardo, we can't burn down the castle. It has a dark protective shield—the moment a flame lands on a wooden beam, heavy rain will pour. So much so, that a natural moat will rise. And, as for your bullets, unless soaked in holy water or blessed by a priest, they will not harm them. They are protected by the power of evil.'

'What about you? Are you protected by these powers?' asks Diabolo.

'No, the moment I saved Alberto, these powers were taken away from me. This is a blessing, as I am no longer on the side of evil. Yes, I am a witch, a good witch, yet young with limited powers, as I need to grow. Enough about me—soon, the evil witches will arise from their evening of drink with a hangover.'

'How much did they have to drink?' asks Mario.

'No more than three glasses of wine,' replies Carlotta with some amusement.

'So, it's true witches can't handle their drink,' says Francesco, whose remark is met with so much laughter that it fills the skyline of the province of Campania.

'Hush, everyone. You will wake the witches. For there is one thing they hate and that is the sound of happiness,' says Carlotta in a low voice.

Nonetheless, Carlotta's words of warning come too late, as suddenly there is a flash of lightning, followed by the roar of thunder. Then, through the air, Carlotta and the rest of the gang hear the chilling and loud voice of the witches' leader Diana. 'Carlotta, Alberto and your friends will perish. An army of goblins has been summoned.'

Carlotta kicks-starts her Lambretta, as do Francesco and Leonardo with their Vespas, as Mario and the rest run towards their cars.

'We must get to Sant' Agata de 'Goti, as the witches have no power there,' orders Carlotta.

'And if we don't?' asks Alberto as he jumps on the back seat of her scooter.

'Then we will all die at the hands of the evil goblins,' replies an alarmed Carlotta.

5

The Great Escape

As the dirt flies off the wheels of Carlotta's Lambretta, Alberto, with all his might, holds onto her waist, for this young fox knows of the legend that an army of blood-thirsty goblins will come to Campania to aid the new Witches of Benevento if they are furious. For this was the prophesy sworn, along with the return of the witches, by Monica to the sky as she was burnt alive at the stake in Sant'Agata de' Goti in 1837. Yet, at the time, her foretelling was jeered at by the baying crowd, as they thought after many centuries of witchcraft being present and powerful in Campania, Monica was just annoyed that she had been caught, after boasting to being a witch during a drunken stupor, so she was bound to say anything in one last attempt to scare the good folk. However, recently many have started to believe that her predictions will come true, as the humans and animals of Campania started to feel a dark force in the air.

As for today, Christmas Eve 1957, the new Witches of Benevento couldn't be more infuriated, as one of their coven, Carlotta, has betrayed them and the fox that was to be sacrificed has escaped with her.

Alberto, now fleeing from the witches of Benevento, is the most petrified he has ever been in his life—even more so than when Napoli was one-nil up against Juventus last year with a minute to go and Juventus had been awarded a penalty. Thankfully for Alberto and the fans of Napoli, Giampiero Boniperti missed, and the whole Stadio Arturo Collana roared, as Napoli were playing at home. Alberto hopes luck like it was then is on his side now.

■ ■ ■

As Carlotta's Lambretta is gathering speed on the winding and dusty road to the sanctuary of Sant'Agata de' Goti from Castello e Torre di Montesarchio, Leonardo and Francesco, the brave and smartly dressed Vespa-riding wolves, overtake her, not as a contest, but to protect her and Alberto from an attack at the front. The silver Alfa Romeo 1900 SS Cabriolet, with Diabolo driving and Mario as a passenger, and the two white Fiat 500 Topolinos with four humans and four foxes, two of each in each car, come up to the rear of Carlotta's Lambretta, again to protect her and the future Don, Alberto.

Whilst the convoy of two wolves, four humans, six foxes, one Doberman and one witch on Italian scooters and cars gathers speed and momentum, 10 grey-fleshed creatures with piercing red eyes wearing tatty and ill-fitting green jackets and trousers in rusty loose-fitting helmets and holding swords leap out in front of the fleet.

Leonardo and Francesco are both respected boxers due to their sheer fearlessness, stamina, technique and strength. They were inspired and trained by their father, Pepe Pugile, the first wolf boxing champion of Naples. In fact, Pepe travelled to New York City in 1948 with his two sons to fight Hans Wolff, a wolf of German descent and the boxing champion of New York City. It was the first-ever transatlantic wolf boxing fight, pioneering the wolf boxing contests across the world that we see today. Pepe won in the third round with a KO punch. After Pepe laid down from his victory exhausted in the changing room, he told his sons to never back down and always launch the first attack.

The two sons are paying heed to the wise words of their very much alive father Pepe, who now runs the best boxing gym in Naples, which has been frequented by Mario, Diabolo, Alberto and the rest of Mario's gang. Yet due to the crisis they are currently facing, no one has spoken about the gym.

'For father!' Leonardo and Francesco howl as they pull back their throttle to achieve maximum acceleration so they can mow down the goblins. The goblins, upon seeing two ferocious yet dapperly dressed wolves on speeding scooters, drop their weapons and flee into the trees that surround the road.

'Cowards!' shouts Leonardo, Francesco following with a loud wolf howl. Diabolo starts honking the horn of the silver Alfa Romeo, as Mario does his best impression of a chicken, whilst the foxes and the humans in the Fiats start to cheer like the penalty miss of Juventus in the final minute of the game against Napoli. Alberto hugs Carlotta around her waist with love, as he is now enjoying his adventure on Christmas Eve.

'We must keep going. Those goblins were just seekers—the worst is yet to come,' yells Carlotta, once everyone has quietened down. The fleet all listen as they all know Carlotta, a child born into magic, is wise to the way witchcraft works, good or bad. So, they keep on going.

'You mean there are more goblins to come?' asks Alberto, who has gone from being triumphant to being scared in less than a minute. 'Many more, but Alberto, like a fox, I am the offspring of the enchanted woods. Now listen: *"Bears of Campania, I ask for your help, the goblins have risen, as have the witches, enemies that have killed and skinned your ancestors, I ask for you to protect us from this evil,"* screeches Carlotta, casting her first-ever spell since leaving the newly formed Witches of Benevento.

Leonardo and Francesco, riding by Carlotta's side, start to howl, not in terms of support, but because the wolves and bears of Campania are not the best of friends. Alberto, oblivious to the wolves' howls, mutters to himself, 'Please help us, bears of Campania.'

Then arrows from the trees start to fly up high and land, which makes the scooters and cars weave in order to avoid this sudden attack.

Carlotta sighs deeply, thinking that her spell may not have worked. Then a beacon of hope appears as the road takes a natural bend to the right, in the form of a small dark stoned church, with a quaint cemetery by its side.

Carlotta rushes through the middle of Leonardo and Francesco, whilst avoiding the onslaught of flying arrows. Carlotta removes her left hand from the handlebars of her Lambretta and with vigour points to the church. Both wolves nod in agreement and follow her, as do the cars. The church is less than 60 seconds away.

Within a minute, all three scooters and three cars park with haste and purpose. The whole convoy now on foot run towards the church. Diabolo cuts in front, bows down his head and rushes towards the old wooden oak door of the church. The full force from the top of his head, a combination of speed and strength, smashes the door open, allowing Carlotta and her new friends into the church and safety.

'Good job those Goblin archers have been out of practice and asleep for over a hundred years. Otherwise, we would all be dead. Well, apart from you, Alberto, as they want to sacrifice you,' says a slightly relieved Carlotta, who is disappointed that her spell to summon the bears of Campania hasn't worked. Alberto doesn't say a word, he just gulps with fear, as he knows that he, his family and friends are still in danger.

Diabolo breaks the silence as he rubs the top of his head, which is throbbing. 'Look, there is a holy water font. Let's dip our bullets in it and take these goblins. I say we creep outside, go up the hills, and attack these creatures from behind. Are you with me?'

'Yes, we are,' Mario's men and foxes shout in unison.

'Diabolo, goblins can be killed by bullets. They don't need to be blessed or dipped in holy water—that is witches. But even a bullet dipped in holy water might just wound them, not kill them. But they are the goblin archers; they come before we face the red cap goblins, caps soaked in the blood of the men and animals they have killed. They are large and strong fiends, with no mercy, who take pleasure in death. I say we leave our vehicles here and sneak into Sant'Agata de' Goti under the cover of the night. We know the village is protected against evil. There, we can plan our next move. We can't act on impulse or retribution, for not only are we saving Alberto, but we are saving the world from an eternity of darkness,' says a confident and thoughtful Carlotta.

Diabolo, experienced in conflict, nods in agreement, as he fondly recalls how he and his troops have taken rivals out by the act of planning. In fact, Sun Tzu's *The Art of War* and Enid Blyton's *The Enchanted Wood* are his favourite books.

'Why haven't the witches attacked us on their broomsticks, with that horrible cat? They were keen enough to kidnap me the other night on them,' asks a bewildered Alberto.

'Maybe one witch will appear on its broomstick. Nonetheless, witches prefer to watch the mayhem from the safety of their castle. Just like the Wicked Witch of the West, with her flying monkeys from *The Wizard of Oz*, but that wasn't Hollywood, that was L. Frank Baum…' Carlotta is cut short.

'Who is L. Frank Baum? That is not a name I have heard around these parts,' asks Franco, a human henchman for Mario.

Carlotta sighs then replies, 'He wrote the book, *The Wizard of Oz*. He was warning the world that witches and witchcraft will rise again. Yet Hollywood turned the book into a fantasy, making the world think it's just make-believe. I bet my last lira witches were involved in the making of that film.'

'So, flying monkeys? They do exist?' asks Marcello, a fox henchman for Mario.

'Yes, but I doubt we will see them, as whenever witches request the services of the flying monkeys, Nikko—their leader in the film and in the real world—will ask for a lot of money. Working in Hollywood has certainly gone to his head. I have a cousin living in Los Angeles—Sophia, a good witch like me. She gives me all the gossip,' says a slightly deflated Carlotta.

'Does she look like Marilyn Monroe, too?' asks Alberto innocently.

'No, Jane Russell,' replies Carlotta with honest delight, making Leonardo and Francesco howl insanely.

'Shut up, you two. Listen to Carlotta, please,' snaps Diabolo, now whole-heartedly supporting her.

'Thank you, Diabolo. I can't hear the sound of flying arrows any more. That means the red-capped goblins will be here soon. We must move quickly,' declares Carlotta.

Suddenly, the ground starts to shake and there is the sound of heavy footsteps approaching the open and broken church door. Leonardo, Francesco, Diabolo, Mario, Carlotta, Alberto and the four foxes and four men all stand to face the forthcoming legion.

'It's the bears of Campania,' screams a delighted Alberto. Carlotta looks to the heavens and blows out a kiss, whilst Leonardo and Francesco tut, and Mario, Diabolo and their gang put their guns by their sides.

One bear dressed in smart jeans and a short-sleeved, light-blue, button-down shirt, holding a sword, steps forward into the church, bends down on one knee and says, 'Madame Carlotta, we are here to protect you and Don Bandito. It is an honour for our gang of 20 bears to serve you, but I have summoned more.'

Following his announcement, the remaining 19 bears smartly dressed in short-sleeved shirts, chinos and jeans walk into the small church, with some holding swords, others holding wooden poles, making it very cramped for everyone in this house of worship.

'What a creep,' whispers Leonardo to Francesco, who then feels a slight punch in his ribs from Carlotta.

'Your band of bears are welcome here. And your name, please?' asks Mario, stepping forward.

'My name is Giorgio Colombo. Me and my two brothers, Giuseppe and Giovanni, are here this evening to serve you. We had the pleasure of painting and decorating your restaurant in the Bay of Naples a few years ago. You paid us well and your wife fed us like kings,' replies Giorgio.

'I bet it was a botched job. Bears are rogues. Remember those bears that pretended to build a wall for Uncle Tommaso?' murmurs Francesco to his brother, Leonardo.

Carlotta turns to face the wolf brothers and with menace says, 'If I hear one more discourteous remark about bears, I will turn the pair of you into toads.' Both Leonardo and Francesco gasp with fright upon hearing Carlotta's threats, even though she hasn't mastered the spell of how to turn wolves into toads yet.

The alert Giorgio, upon hearing the slight commotion between the witch and the two wolves, gets up from one knee, turns to all three, and politely says, 'Leonardo and Francesco, the wolf champion boxers from Benevento, it is an honour to meet you.'

Giorgio's comments make both the wolf brothers break into beaming smiles. Carlotta slightly chuckles, knowing that Giorgio's flattering remark has boosted the wolves' egos, therefore making them more acceptable to the bears, who are here to fight with them against the goblins.

'Oh yes, the Colombo Brothers: a name that is respected in Naples as master craft bears. Once we have overcome this slight problem, I will certainly use your services again, but first we must leave this church and by foot get to Sant'Agata de' Goti for safety,' declares an authoritative Mario, as his right-hand dog Diabolo stands by his side, nodding his sore head in agreement.

Giorgio bows down his head upon hearing the approval and orders from Don Mario.

Carlotta walks up to Mario and asks, 'May I?' Mario says nothing, but just nods, as he knows this witch has their safety, especially his son's, in her heart.

'We are less than 10 minutes away from the protection of Sant'Agata de' Goti. By my side, I want Francesco, Leonardo, Diabolo, Giorgio, Giuseppe and Giovanni. Behind us, the army of bears, and behind them, Mario and his men. With Alberto in the middle, we will create a wall: one witch, one dog, two wolves, 20 bears, five foxes, plus Alberto and four humans. I can sense that the bloodthirsty red-capped goblins will be outside waiting for us. Yet from my learnings, they might be ruthless but they are not fearless. We are brave, we are strong, we will defeat this evil,' orders Carlotta like a true warrior.

Her words are met with roars, howls and cheers, as she leads her brave army into certain battle.

When Carlotta, with her new brave and loyal legion steps out of the church and into the yard, they are greeted by what they had been expecting: 30 or so human-size goblins in red caps, dressed in light armour, holding battleaxes, and above them, hovering on a broomstick, is the mystic-looking Andriana.

Andriana and Carlotta exchange evil glares, with Andriana yelling: 'Traitor!' Carlotta laughs and replies, 'No, I saw the light, and at least I don't look like a cheap fairground fortune teller.'

Andriana hisses, then says: 'Give us the young fat fox and I will spare your lives.' The red cap goblins start to stamp their feet hard on the ground as they wave their axes, believing this gesture will intimidate Carlotta's troops. Yet these animals and humans from Campania are fearless and strong—and are willing to risk their lives for a noble cause.

Carlotta stands with her head held high and with pride, she states, 'Spare our lives? Ha. You sound like the Wicked Witch of the West from The Wizard of Oz. Andriana, not only do you have the dress sense of many centuries ago, but also your weapons haven't moved with the times. You have axes… and… we… have…'

'Guns,' screeches Diabolo right on cue on Carlotta's declaration, pulling out his pistol from his once nice but now battered three-button light brown suit. Diabolo fires the first shot at a red cap goblin. The bullet skims the top of the goblin's head, causing him no harm, but his beloved red cap flies off, making the nasty creature scream.

'Yes, but we have fire from Hell,' screams Andriana, as she pulls out a glass ball from a black leather satchel bag hanging over her left shoulder. With all her strength, as Andriana is incredibly strong, she throws the ball into the group of bears. As the ball lands, there is an almighty sound, like the eruption of a volcano, followed by a red flash that lights up the sky, then flames burst out making the bears flee for safety, as they fear burning alive.

Marcello, known around Naples as a good shot, points his rifle and fires at the witch, hitting her upon impact, yet not hurting Andriana. 'Stupid fox, your bullets can't harm me. Take this,' says Andriana, and from her bag she throws a small piece of string at Marcello. As the string gets closer to the fox, it turns into a king cobra snake. Marcello screams, drops his gun and runs back into the church, as he is chased by the venomous snake.

'Mario and your gang, go into the church, save Marcello. Alberto—go with your father,' orders Carlotta. Then she whispers to Diabolo: 'Now, dip your bullets into the holy water font.' Then she returns to her normal authoritative voice in this current situation: 'But leave two armed foxes or men here. Giorgio, go and find your bears. Francesco, Leonardo, Giuseppe and Giovanni, stand with me'.

Carlotta's diminished gang now face a smug-looking Andriana, flying on her broomstick above the fierce-looking and battle-ready red cap goblins—one without a cap, due to Diablo's bullet. Carlotta had not anticipated that her adversary Andriana would be here, along with a bag of spells from Hell.

'Carlotta, I offer this to you one last time: give me the fat fox, Alberto, or my goblins will hack you and your friends to death. You know that your guns are no match for me and my magic. Surrender, Carlotta, while you still have the chance,' says a sinister and triumphant Andriana.

Carlotta wipes away a tear, looks at Francesco, Leonardo, Giuseppe and Giovanni, and says: 'We can't lose, we just can't.'

Andriana, upon hearing the one-time member of the new Witches of Benevento, cackles just like a witch does and says, 'Looks like you have.'

6

The Battle of Sant'Agata de' Goti

Upon hearing the conceited tone of Andriana's declaration, Carlotta glances at Francesco and Leonardo, and says, 'Which one of you fancies your chances then?'

Leonardo, the elder of the brothers, slowly takes off his three-button tailor-made jacket, neatly folds it, places the item of clothing slowly on the ground, then valiantly declares, 'I do.'

Then the fearless wolf runs towards the red-capped goblins, who quickly disperse upon seeing the oncoming, scary-looking animal. Andriana gazes at Leonardo with astonishment, which turns to shock as Leonardo leaps high into the air, grabbing the front handle of Andriana's broomstick.

'Get off me, you crazy filthy wolf,' Andriana screams, yet the courageous and strong Leonardo shakes her broomstick so hard in mid-air, regardless of his own safety. Leonardo has one thing on his mind—for Andriana to drop her leather satchel of spells.

His bravery pays off, as he rattles the flying broomstick so hard that Andriana has no choice but to use both her arms to steady it, allowing the bag to slide all the way down her left arm and into the cypress trees sloping on the roadside.

'No!' screams Andriana, as she sees her weapons of mayhem drop with so much force that they break many branches before hitting the dusty and hard soil, which explodes upon impact.

As the blaze shoots up in between the trees, Leonardo, in mid-air and still holding onto the broomstick, pulls himself towards it, pushes his head back, then somersaults backwards to the safety of the road. The blast and Leonardo's backflip make everyone, from Carlotta's small gang to the bloodthirsty red-capped goblins, gasp loudly—well, apart from Andriana, who bolts off her broomstick,

as the leaping flames hit her backside, which makes her do a somersault, too. Yet unlike Leonardo's landing, which would have certainly won the wolf a gold medal in gymnastics, Andriana lands awkwardly on her knees, shrieking out in pain as she hits the ground.

Andriana gets up, brushes herself off, looks with pure hatred at Leonardo, who is standing proud. She turns to the confused and simple red-capped goblins, and orders, 'Kill the others, leave the grubby wolf to me.'

The red-capped goblins—and the one goblin without his cap, due to being shot off by Diabolo—hold their axes towards the Moon, as they yell, 'Kill! Kill! Kill!'

Giuseppe bravely stands in front of Carlotta, whilst holding his sword with determination, looks to the skies, and shouts out, 'Brother bears of Campania, we do not flee from fire. I order you to return—we must fight this evil.'

'Save your words, Teddy. Your fur will be my blanket tonight when I go to sleep after slaughtering you with my axe,' gurgles a vicious voice from a revolting red-capped goblin. Giuseppe looks at his attacker, showing no fear, yet hoping that his pleas are answered.

■ ■ ■

Leonardo looks at the war-torn Andriana and calmly says, 'You have no spells. There is nothing you can do to harm me. Walk now, before I knock you down.'

'Ha, I know you, your brother and your father Pepe—amateur boxers. Come on, you won't make it to the first bell,' says a rather confident Andriana, as she takes up the orthodox stance of boxing.

Because, unknown to Leonardo, as Andriana waited to find a coven to practise her evil magic, she sought employment as a fortune teller with a travelling fair, which is one of the main reasons why she still dresses like one. Yet Andriana lacked people skills and still does, so her booth was always empty. Therefore, she learnt how to box and became the boxing champion of the fair, thus Andriana was able to pay her bills. Yes, witches do pay their way.

Going back to the fairground boxing, men would foolishly embarrass themselves in front of their family or lovers, as they lost their lira, believing that they could last three rounds with the traditional gypsy-looking woman. Andriana won all her fights with a KO in the first round.

Leonardo, born into boxing, knows straight away from Andriana's posture that she is no amateur. So, he rolls up his now slightly singed and dirty white shirt sleeves and takes up his trademark Southpaw stance.

Andriana and Leonardo, like all boxers at the start of a fight, approach each other with caution, slowly weaving their arms, waiting for that opening. Leonardo then takes it upon himself to launch the first attack, coming in with three fast jabs, yet Andriana bobs and weaves and replies with a right uppercut to Leonardo's stomach, who moves slightly, so the punch doesn't wind him, and retaliates with a left hook. Experienced in the noble art of boxing as Andriana is, she is nevertheless too slow to block or avoid the oncoming punch that hits her hard in the side of the ribs.

Leonardo rather foolishly believes that his one punch will put the seasoned boxer Andriana out of action. Yet she laughs at Leonardo when his paw lands on her body, 'Ha! Is that all you have got, Wolfie?'

Then she strikes back with a left uppercut that hits Leonardo hard on his big black snout. Leonardo's eyes start to water from the punch, slightly blocking his vision, as Andriana comes in with a classic left hook that hits the wolf on the side of his head. Yet with his back legs firmly anchored to the ground, Leonardo sways a great deal but doesn't go down. Like Leonardo with his left hook, Andriana doesn't follow through, as she feels she has done enough to knock the wolf out.

Leonardo doesn't waste his energy or time by taunting his opponent, instead, he replies by a jab left hook-cross with power and speed, enough to put Andriana on her backside.

'You nasty wolf,' she bellows as she hits the ground. Leonardo, a devout devotee of the Queensberry rules, stands over Andriana, as he loudly counts to 10.

'One, two, three, four… ouch!' he says, as by the time Leonardo gets to five, Andriana raises her right leg and kicks Leonardo in a painful part of his body. He leaps up into the air, then falls to the floor on his right side. Seeing her opponent down, Andriana, with all her might, pushes herself up, then quickly bends over to pick up the biggest rock she can find and makes her way to kill the lying wolf.

∎ ∎ ∎

'Then your axe will have to kill 20 bears!' shouts Giuseppe to the red cap goblin, as he points to the bears of Campania running back to the church, after nearly being burnt alive by the fires of Hell.

'You forgot about the foxes and humans with guns!' is shouted out, as Diabolo,

Alberto, Mario, Marcello, who is holding a dead king cobra snake, and the rest of the gang gloriously march out of the church.

'And the villagers!' shouts out a gratified Alberto, who sees a large crowd of humans, foxes and dogs carrying torches, coming down the hill of Sant'Agata de' Goti.

The red-capped goblins look at Mario and Carlotta's small army then at the angry villagers, who are now shouting 'Kill the witch! Kill the goblins!', and scream 'Run!', dropping their axes as they flee.

'Shall we give chase, Madame Carlotta?' asks Giorgio.

'No, let's get Alberto and all of us to the safety of Sant'Agata de' Goti,' says a battle-tired Carlotta. Carlotta's words are greeted by loud cheers, and due to all the commotion, everyone has forgotten about the boxing match between the wolf and the witch.

Suddenly, out of the corner of his eye, Diabolo sees Andriana holding a rock above her head, as she stands over the collapsed Leonardo. Quickly, like a Sheriff from a Wild West film, Diabolo pulls out his pistol and shoots Andriana in the backside with a bullet he had dipped in the holy water font in the church.

Andriana screams out and drops the rock as she feels a sharp pain in her backside. Andriana, who was so engrossed in killing off Leonardo, has just noticed that the red-capped goblins have absconded. She now knows that she is greatly outnumbered and powerless. Consequently, Andriana puts her index finger and thumb into her mouth and whistles. Her flying broomstick miraculously appears under the moonlight, then glides down to her waist. Andriana gets onto the broomstick, shakes her fist with anger towards Carlotta and Alberto, then flies off into the night.

'Kill her, Diabolo!' shouts out Marcello.

'No, not in front of Alberto,' Carlotta harshly orders.

'Yes, let her go. We will get the witch another day. Let's go to Sant'Agata de' Goti, so we can celebrate the night before Christmas,' says Mario, as he too doesn't want his beloved son to witness death.

Mario's words are greeted with a loud ovation from his gang and the bears, as Alberto starts to do a bop dance, much to the delight of everyone.

'We welcome you, Don Bandito, to Sant'Agata de' Goti,' says a rather authoritative voice over the celebrations.

Mario, taking his role as the leader, holds his paws above his head then brings them down, making the commemorations suddenly cease. Mario turns to face a portly well-dressed man with a big thick black moustache.

'I am Enzo Robotti, the head villager. My great, great, grandfather, Gianni Robotti, was the head villager who brought about the end of the reign of terror our ancestors experienced when the Witches of Benevento walked amongst us. Please follow us back to our humble town, where we will prepare a feast. We will open our homes for you to have a bath, and there is a bed this evening for everyone, and tomorrow, the whole village and all of you will celebrate Christmas in our piazza.'

Everyone, from the villagers to the bears of Campania, applauds the loudest they have ever applauded in their life as they follow Enzo Robotti and Mario back to Sant'Agata de' Goti.

■ ■ ■

'Mamma, I am safe,' says a jubilant Alberto on the telephone in the booth in Lorenzo's pizzeria in Sant'Agata de' Goti, owned and run by Salvatore Cameriere—a fluffy white Maremma Sheepdog, whose grandfather Paride started working here many years ago as a waiter, because Paride couldn't abide working with sheep any more. Yet it didn't take long for Paride to master the art of cooking the perfect pizza. It is a skill he passed down to his first-born son, Lorenzo, who bought the pizzeria just after the war, then retired and passed his heritage onto Salvatore, who is perhaps the best pizza chef in the whole of Campania. All the pizzerias for miles around have tried to lure Salvatore, but so far, Salvatore has not been tempted, as he loves this village and the thought of living and working in Naples frightens this pleasant and talented dog.

Alberto jumped for joy when he realised that he and Diabolo would be staying at the flat above Lorenzo's pizzeria and Salvatore would cook them a pizza to see Christmas Day in. However, like any loving son, he wanted to call his mother from the pizzeria's telephone booth, to let her know he is safe, as three hours ago, Alberto thought he would never see his mother again.

Silvia falls to her knees on hearing her son's high-pitched sweet voice. 'Alberto, I knew you would be safe—you're a Bandito, a good family name. Your safety is the best present that I could ever have.'

Alberto feels the love from his mother over the telephone and starts to cry so much that he passes the telephone receiver over to Mario, who is standing behind his son.

'Silvia, call Vincenzo. Arrange for him to bring you here this evening. Tell him, I want 20 armed foxes and men and they must dip their bullets in the nearest holy water font. Get a convoy of seven cars and for you to be in the middle car. I and the rest of my foxes and men will head to Naples to meet you on the route. I can safely leave Alberto here with Diabolo to watch over our son.'

'Yes, Mario, I will call Vincenzo now. See you soon. Bye! I love you,' says a joyous and highly relieved Silvia, as she is looking forward to spending the remainder of Christmas Eve and Christmas Day with her son and husband in a beautiful village filled with love and happiness.

Mario, and his gang of four foxes and four humans, say their goodbyes and leave to meet Silvia so they can escort her from Naples to Sant'Agata de' Goti. Just before Mario's departure, Salvatore and Diabolo promise to keep an eye on Alberto, who is now having his best Christmas Eve ever.

As Alberto tucks into another slice of pizza, he is pleased to see three of the bears of Campania—the brothers Giorgio, Giuseppe and Giovanni Colombo—along with the two wolf brothers from Benevento—Leonardo and Francesco Pugile—walk in, all laughing and joking.

'I see you are friends now,' says the happy Alberto.

'When you stand by a man, fox, wolf or bear in a battle against evil, you become friends for life,' says a rather jolly but slightly punch-drunk Leonardo.

'Salvatore, five gorgonzola and cipolla pizzas, please,' says Giorgio.

'Please take a seat with Signor Alberto and Signor Diabolo. I will bring you the finest pizzas you have ever tasted,' says the overworked, yet still remaining happy Salvatore, with his wife Monica, a Maremma Sheepdog, coming out from the kitchen to lay yet another place at the table.

Alberto looks at Leonardo and Francesco then with innocence says, 'I thought wolves were children of the night. My father always quoted Bela Lugosi when we saw a wolf walking through Naples.'

'Ha, Bela Lugosi, the man was too chicken to answer the door when our father Pepe turned up at his house in Hollywood,' says a rather annoyed Francesco. 'Yes Alberto, our family and all wolves across the world hate that line as it makes everyone think that wolves are evil. We are still speaking to a New York lawyer about suing Bela Lugosi and the director Todd Browning for discrimination against wolves. Wolves, like the fox and the bear, are children of nature, not the night. As everyone knows, a wolf loves a good night's sleep!' says Leonardo, ending his sentence on a positive note, so the festive spirit can continue.

'Oh, I see… Where's Carlotta?' asks Alberto, suddenly realising the hero who saved him is nowhere to be seen.

'Don't worry, she is literally outside, talking to some menfolk,' reassures Giovanni, as he helps himself to a few breadsticks before his pizza.

'Thank you, Giovanni,' says Alberto, as he rushes out to find his new best friend Carlotta.

Carlotta is casually sitting on the historical wall, as two handsome men from Sant'Agata de' Goti are desperately trying to get her attention, which doesn't surprise Alberto, as she surely is Italy's answer to Marilyn Monroe. The two local men, upon seeing the son and heir to a Don approaching, politely say 'Hello,' wish him Merry Christmas and depart with haste.

'I am sorry to scare your admirers away. Shall I go and say they can come back?' Carlotta chuckles and opens her arms for Alberto to jump into them, so they can hug, which they do with pure affection.

'Thank you for saving me and giving me the best Christmas ever,' says a happy Carlotta.

'How did I save you?' asks the ever-curious Alberto.

'When I saw you at the market in October...'

Yet Carlotta is cut short by a rather excited Alberto: 'I remember now, seeing you. I really thought Marilyn Monroe was in Naples that day.'

'Oh, bless you, Alberto. When I saw you laughing and just loving life, it dawned on me that I wasn't evil. I know I am a witch; I have known that since the age of three, but I was a witch on the wrong path. I had briefly succumbed to evil. But after seeing you, the jolly young fox, I told the coven I had to return home to curse a farmer who was trying to buy my poor aunt's land.

'Yet I didn't return home, I caught the ferry to Sardinia, where I knew I would be alone and at one with nature. Under the shining stars, I called out to my ancestors find out who I am. Alberto, I descend from a long line of good witches who are guardians of nature and warriors against evil. I am the last of my heritage in human form. It was my great-great-great-grandmother Luna who gave Jasper Ludham the power to walk and talk like man, as she knew powerful foxes would bring beauty and love to this world.'

'Oh, gosh,' exclaims Alberto.

'"Oh, gosh" indeed. Once I found out who I am, I asked about the curse of "i sogni dei bambini". When I learnt it is a prophecy that darkness will rule the world, I then knew it was my destiny to stop it. When Ettore lured you out of your home, did he scratch you?' asks Carlotta worriedly.

'Yes, that fathead of a cat did. Look, I still have the mark on the side of my left cheek,' roars an annoyed Alberto.

'Then you are cursed by the witches and they won't stop until they have sacrificed you,' says Carlotta.

'Oh no! Can't you break the curse?' says Alberto, who is now naturally worried upon hearing this revelation.

'I can't. It has to be another fox. I said I was the last of my heritage as a human, but there is the last of my heritage as a fox. The only problem is that she doesn't know she is a witch—well, not yet. But she can break the curse and… save the world,' says Carlotta, as she offers support to her furry friend.

'Find her and my father will pay her whatever it costs, or we will kidnap her friends,' declares the son of the Don.

'Alberto, your father's code will not work. We need to go to a little village called Foxham in Norfolk, England.'

'My father and mother have been to Foxham, but I was too young to travel with them,' boasts Alberto.

'That's nice. In Foxham, there is an ancient manuscript and a bottle of liquid magic from Barbagia, Sardinia. A fox called Trudi Milanesi, originally from Milan, must use them to lift the curse. Trudi left Italy just after the war with her grandmother, who is also a witch, but lacks the magic. She and her grandmother now run a care home for injured foxes and a cafe in the village.'

'But she is from Milan. My father says: never trust a Milanese,' proclaims Alberto.

Carlotta, now slightly laughing, says: 'Forget your regional prejudice.'

'What?' asks a confused Alberto.

'It means disliking someone just because they come from a different place than you,' states Carlotta.

'Oh, I see,' snaps Alberto.

'Now, please listen, Alberto, and don't say another word. This is important. After Christmas, you and your family must flee Naples and head to Foxham. You will have to stay there until Easter Sunday, the 6th April. Then on the evening of that day, you will have to go to the turret of the old medieval tower on Foxham Common, lay on your back to face the moon, and have the bottle of liquid blue magic poured over you. Next, Trudi will read from the ancient manuscript at one minute to midnight, the curse will be broken, and the witches and their allies finished. But as the portal of magic is open the witches can overcome Trudi, sacrifice you at the same place at the same time, and if they do, then we have truly lost. They are getting stronger. Tonight, we fought a feeble army, but in a week or two, the witches will be sturdier. Mario will have to leave many of his gang here, to guard the region, but they can't know about the prophecy or they will be too scared to protect Naples and beyond,' says a reflective Carlotta.

Alberto gulps then replies, 'Oh my. I just thought they were mean witches. Will you come to England with me, please?'

'Alberto, I am your friend and your guardian. I will be by your side until then,' says Carlotta.

'So, after 6th April, you will not be my friend any more?' asks a now saddened Alberto.

'I am your friend for life. Now, come on, let's enjoy Christmas. Soon your mother will be here and we will have a good celebration. That pizza sure smells good.'

'Yes,' shouts out Alberto, as he jumps into the air.

7

Trudi Milanesi and Charlie the Rebel

'You are a wicked little fox, Charlie Renard. You are a disgrace to all the foxes of Foxham,' screams the usually kind-hearted and caring Trudi Milanesi, a jolly and slightly plump fox who left Italy as a cub after the war with her grandmother Anna after her husband and Trudi's grandfather Silvio passed away.

• • •

Anna and Silvio were the humble yet successful owners of a quaint and elegant hotel with a restaurant in the Porta Magenta district of Milan called Silvio's Palazzo. The hotel boasted 14 luxurious rooms, with king-size beds and bathrooms en suite, whereas the restaurant served delicious, traditional and home-made Italian food that was a 'must' for the whole of Milan. The footballing stars of AC and Inter Milan would always put their football rivalry aside when they dined at Silvio's Palazzo, as it was a restaurant filled with love and laughter as everyone, from the stars to the delivery foxes, enjoyed Anna Milanesi's scrumptious cooking. What is more, it was in the kitchen of Silvio's Palazzo that the young Trudi first felt happiness and devotion.

Trudi was the only cub born to Gigi and Lucinda Milanesi. Sadly for Trudi, her parents did not shower her with love and affection, the reason being that Gigi wanted his firstborn to be a son and heir.

Gigi, after seeing Lucinda give birth to a female cub on 1st September 1936, swore then and there in the hospital that there would be no more cubs, and that his only daughter would be raised as a servant and her name would be Schiava. Fortunately for Trudi, Gigi's parents Anna and Silvio were in the same hospital room visiting when Trudi was born as he made this nasty and vile declaration.

Anna looked at her son and said with tears and anger that she and Silvio would name her Trudi and raise the cub as their own. Gigi turned his back on his own mother and said: 'Take her. I never want to see her again.' Anna and Silvio picked up Trudi and stormed out of the hospital room. To this day, Trudi and her father have seldom spoken to each other.

Anna knew the moment her granddaughter was born that she was a good witch, as Anna is, too, yet the magic is not powerful within her soul. Furthermore, Anna is wary of her own son, who sold his soul a long time ago. Therefore, he detests anything natural, beautiful and bright. That is why he rejected his daughter on sight and Anna knew Trudi needed protection from this evil and the possibility of a war looming.

■ ■ ■

After the war, like many young folks, Trudi had a happy cubhood, popular at school with her peers of children, fox cubs and one bear cub, Marco.

Trudi, due to her strong and confident personality with empathy, quickly emerged as a leader in the classroom and the playground, often bringing order when her friends were being disruptive, much to the delight of the human teachers and one fox teacher. Her popularity was heightened due to her excellent skills as a goalkeeper in football.

In fact, it was in this sport that her competitive nature shone through. A friendly football match against a nearby school, where the parents were wealthy and spoilt their little angels, was being played in a park, with parents, pupils, a few locals and teachers watching. Yet Trudi, in goal, and her team knew it wasn't a friendly match, as they believed the wealthy school had paid the referee, Armando Ferrario, a banker, to fix the match, as two of her team had been sent off and Trudi saved seven penalties from questionable decisions.

In the last minute at nil-nil, Trudi had a goal kick, she looked at her grandparents and friends at the side of the pitch and decided to win the match. So, the gallant Trudi, instead of kicking the ball, chose to dribble past the opposing team with much ease and the moment she got within three feet of their goalkeeper, she toe-poked the ball between his legs and into the back of the net. All her family, friends, school and the locals cheered; the referee, Armando Ferrario, left the pitch and has not been seen since.

But it was in the kitchen, helping her grandmother out, that Trudi was at peace as she learned the art of Italian cuisine.

When Silvio suddenly passed away, Gigi took over Silvio's Palazzo, as instructed in Silvio's will. Anna was convinced it was a forgery, but she was unable to prove it. So, she along with her granddaughter, decided to leave Italy in 1951.

Anna and Trudi headed to Foxham, Norfolk, England. She, Silvio and Trudi had met Charles and Kaye Renard when they spent two weeks at Silvio's Palazzo a few years ago. Charles said he would always help the Milanesis out if they needed it and Anna knew wholeheartedly that Charles meant it.

■ ■ ■

Anna was right, Charles is a fox of his word. He gave Anna and Trudi the responsibility of running a care home for injured foxes, Foxham Care Home for Foxes, where many foxes have come and gone after getting better—well, apart from Chester Brown, a fox who turned up a few years ago with amnesia and a badly injured left leg. To this date, Chester is still a resident, even though he no longer has amnesia, but he swears blind that he still has trouble walking.

Charles was also generous to loan Anna and Trudi the money at no interest so they could purchase the local baker's, Loaves, a shop on Foxham High Road that looks out onto the common. The original owner, Eric Stills, and his wife Joan, humans, decided to move to the coast for their retirement. The village gave him and his wife a big send-off, with Charles giving them a very large cash donation.

Loaves had been a popular part of the community, and Charles knew Anna and Trudi would carry on the legacy. Changing the name to Milano's, Anna and Trudi kept on the traditional British side of the bakery, from sausage rolls to Victoria sponge. But slowly and surely, they started to introduce Italian food: pizza, rice balls, lasagne and such like. At first, all the locals—humans, dogs, foxes and badgers—were apprehensive to sample 'foreign muck', as they once called it, but now they love Italian food. Milano's has become a huge success in Foxham and it didn't take long for Anna to pay Charles his money back.

∎ ∎ ∎

For many years, there has been harmony in Foxham between the foxes, humans, dogs and badgers, even though every now and then drunk humans, mainly from Norwich, drive through Foxham and shout out 'Tally Ho' to the foxes—the biggest insult you can say to a fox. Yet all the villagers always unite to chase these troublesome men out of their picturesque village.

However, like all villages in England, there is the odd bit of trouble with their own, and in Foxham, the biggest troublemaker of all is Charlie Renard, grandson of Charles and son of Foxham's own 'ducker and diver' Ferdy Renard.

Charlie, influenced by rock 'n' roll music, fashion and American comics, decided to form a gang, 'The Young Rascals', at the start of this spring to cause trouble, with him as the leader, dressing like the recently departed James Dean from *Rebel Without A Cause* in a red Baracuta G9 jacket, white tee shirt and blue jeans. Fortunately for Foxham, The Young Rascals only has three members: two snotty and scruffy nosed human kids, Matthew Wright and Billy Wells, who foolishly idolise Charlie; and the gullible and easily manipulated Owen Cambridge—the youngest cub to library owner Oliver Cambridge and Victoria Cambridge, the editor of the local newspaper, *The Foxham Gazette*, and brother to the studious, smartly dressed and pleasant Thomas. They are a respected and liked fox family from Foxham.

Most of the time, the adults and the younger folk of Foxham take no notice of Charlie, aged 13, and his gang, as they have found they are easy to chase off. In fact, The Young Rascals are more of an annoyance than an actual threat to the village. This frustrates Charlie no end, as he wants to be public enemy number one, not just in Foxham but the whole of Norfolk. Until Charlie receives the notoriety he feels he deserves, he and his gang will carry on being a pest around the township.

One day during this summer of 1957, Charlie and The Young Rascals tried to build a raft by the Norfolk Broads that run behind Foxham Woods, for Charlie had this idea they could build a raft and float off to America by teatime. But when he and his gang saw that this plan was not going to work, they decided to go to Foxham Common, with their catapults and pea-shooters. Knowing that Milano's at present was out of bounds, as Trudi had banned them, they set their sights on Thomas Cambridge, in his white shirt and green shorts, sitting underneath the shade of the oak tree, reading a book about the Battle of Waterloo, as Thomas has an interest in history and the strategy of warfare.

Thomas takes a break from reading, so he can enjoy his packed lunch of home-made Jubilee chicken sandwiches, a pork pie from Milano's (his favourite), a packet of plain crisps with a blue packet of salt for Thomas to add and shake, a slice of apple pie (again from Milano's) and a bottle of home-made lemonade. As Thomas wets his lips and is about to bite into his sandwich, Charlie sneaks up from behind and snatches the food from out of his paw. 'Gee, that's swell, T,' says Charlie, trying to sound like a kid from America.

Charlie's sudden antics make the rest of The Young Rascals giggle, including Thomas's younger brother Owen. Thomas has no fear of confronting Charlie, Matthew and Billy, yet to see his brother join in with this horrible teasing makes Thomas burst into tears. As Thomas starts to wail due to a broken heart, the rest of The Young Rascals start to laugh—well, apart from Owen, who suddenly realises that he has done wrong, and he loves his brother much more than Charlie.

Trudi, adding mushrooms to her popular pizzas in Milano's before the teatime rush, as Anna is looking after the fox patients at the care home, hears the cries of Thomas, a fox she is very fond of. To her horror, she sees Charlie Renard, Matthew Wright, Billy Wells and his own brother mocking Thomas. Annoyed and ready to fight every member of The Young Rascals, Trudi runs out of Milano's to save the distressed young fox.

'Scram! That dame ain't nothing but trouble,' says Charlie, in the worst attempt at an American accent you are ever going to hear in your life. Like the followers they are, Matthew and Billy follow Charlie as he runs into Foxham Woods to escape the wrath of Trudi.

Nevertheless, Owen decides to stay with his upset brother. Owen walks over to comfort his brother; they hug as Owen also bursts into tears.

Trudi stops running as she gets to Thomas and Owen, comforting each other under the oak tree on Foxham Common and shouts out, 'You are a wicked little fox,

Charlie Renard. You are a disgrace to all the foxes of Foxham.' Unlike her grand-mother Anna, Trudi doesn't have an Italian accent any more.

So, dear readers, we are back to the start of this chapter, the summer of 1957 in Foxham, six months before the abduction of Alberto Bandito by the Witches of Benevento.

■ ■ ■

'I am here to arrest Charlie Jasper Renard for theft,' declares an assertive Sergeant Ali, the German Shepherd police dog, son of the one-time Sergeant Brutus, who moved from Boxworth to Foxham after he got promoted in 1947. Sergeant Ali is standing at the large doors of Fox Hill Hall, along with his new recruits, PC Bryan, a human, and PC Rex, another German Shepherd, recently transferred from Bethnal Green.

After the war, the British government insisted that all criminal matters in the villages would not be dealt with by the head of the village like Charles anymore, but by a magistrate; and in Foxham, that role belongs to Penelope Painshill, a ruthless fox, who along with her somewhat buffoonish husband Sebastian (who can always be found at the local tavern, The Six Bells) and her two cubs, Henry, a snooty little fox, and Isabella, a carefree fox, moved to Foxham in 1954 from Cobham, Surrey.

'Sergeant Ali, you are aware that you are saying that Charles Renard's grandson is a common thief. Be gone with your lies, be gone while you still have a job,' says the annoyed and now older Boris Bates, Charles' butler, friend and advisor.

'Boris, yesterday, Ronald Blades the butcher, after visiting his sick mother, re-ported 24 sausages missing, along with 5Ibs of mince, 10 steaks, and some ham and pork. So, we made some enquiries around the village and this morning, Mrs Duke states that she saw Charlie Renard and Owen Cambridge go into the butcher's empty-handed, but both came out with one heavy sack each,' declares Sergeant Ali.

Boris starts to chuckle, which annoys Sergeant Ali a great deal. 'Officer, his mother is as fit as a fiddle and Mrs Duke is still upset that Hitler didn't win the war. Look at the size of Charlie and little Owen. Carrying that amount of meat for them is impossible. You jest like an out-of-work court jester.'

'Boris, I do not want to arrest you for obstructing a police dog in his duty, but I will if I have to,' snaps Sergeant Ali. Boris, fiercely loyal to the Renards, puffs out his chest and stands in the entrance of the manor house, blocking the police dogs and policeman from entering.

As devoted as he is to Charles and his family, Boris is not a bachelor badger. He and his wife Wilma and their two daughters, Maria and Nancy, live in a cosy cottage in the grounds of Fox Hill Hall, where Wilma runs a successful bookkeeping company for the shops and businesses in Foxham.

'Boris, please move out of the way or you're nicked,' snaps the always-aggressive London dog, PC Rex, who misses his beat on the streets of East London, where scraps and backhanders were an everyday occurrence.

'Listen, you cockney dog, your threats do not scare me, do your worst... you steamer!' yells Boris, ready for the confrontation.

PC Rex, relishing the opportunity for a punch-up, throws off his helmet and steps forward. 'No, PC Rex, we are here to do it by the book,' orders Sergeant Ali. PC Rex puts his head down and starts to whimper like a pet dog used to.

'Boris, let the police in. I am sure we can clear this up,' says Ferdy, approaching the hallway of Fox Hill Hall from the drawing-room.

Unlike his brother Foxy and his family, Ferdy has not left home. Foxy and his wife Sandy, and their two cubs, Hector and Arnold, still live in Foxham, yet Ferdy and his wife Doris and their only son Charlie have decided not to vacate Fox Hill Hall. It's not because Ferdy feels a strong sense of loyalty to his father and mother, Kaye; no, it's to save money. However, Ferdy is not overly cautious with money, it's just he would rather spend his cash on sports cars, Italian clothes, posh restaurants and holidays in Paris—in fact, on anything luxurious other than buying a house or contributing to society.

Ferdy made a small fortune during the war as a spiv and he still operates in the black market to this day. As a cover, he runs a popular fish and chip shop in Foxham, yet every year, he tells the taxman he hasn't made any money. Ferdy has not paid any tax since 1939, the year Great Britain went to war.

'Thank you, Mr Ferdy,' says Sergeant Ali, as Boris reluctantly steps aside, allowing Sergeant Ali, PC Bryan and PC Rex into the hallway. Sergeant Ali observes Ferdy in his light chino trousers and lilac shirt, believing that Ferdy might be behind this robbery so he could sell the meat around the watering holes of Norfolk—well, apart from The Six Bells, as his ban for life was reintroduced the following day after Charles' meeting with Winston Churchill.

'Sergeant Ali, you are welcome. Why don't you and your officers come in, and put your paws and feet up? Have a nice glass of ale or wine, have some roast chicken, relax, and I will donate a large amount of cash that you can give to a charity of your choice,' suggests a rather sly Ferdy.

'Mr Ferdy, are you trying to bribe a police dog? I will arrest you if you offer that to me again. Now, PC Rex go up and arrest Charlie Renard,' snaps the irritated Sergeant Ali.

'Your father never said no to a cash donation,' yells Ferdy, who hates it when things don't go his way.

'Right, that's it. Cuff him, PC Bryan. I am arresting you for trying to bribe a police dog,' barks Sergeant Ali.

'Yes, sarge,' says PC Bryan.

'I am Charles Renard's son, I run this village,' declares Ferdy.

'You run nothing, you muttonhead,' shouts Charles, with Kaye and Charlie coming down the spectacular velvet carpeted staircase of Fox Hill Hall with its carved oak banisters.

'Oh no, it's the cops. I ain't going to no Sing Sing,' says Charlie, sounding like a fifth-rate James Cagney impersonation.

'Charlie, you do not come from New York. Speak in your proper accent,' orders Kaye.

Charlie puts his head down, sobs, and says, 'Sorry, grandmother, but I didn't steal anything. Please, I am innocent.'

'We will have to let the police do their duty, Charlie. I am sorry, but that is the law, it's the agreement I made with Winston Churchill. Sergeant Ali, you can take my son and grandson away. But I and Boris will come with you, just to make sure everything is done correctly and my grandson is treated well'

'What about me?' cries Ferdy.

'Ferdy, please, Foxham police cells are your second home,' sighs Charles.

'Thank you, Sir Charles. As you know, PC Rex will have to search Charlie's bedroom—that is the protocol,' says Sergeant Ali, now in control of the situation.

'Go to the top of the stairs, turn left, walk straight down the hall and you will find his bedroom, PC Rex,' says a resigned Charles.

With great delight, PC Rex rushes to the top of the stairs, whilst Charles turns to Sergeant Ali and says, 'What about Owen Cambridge? Have you arrested him yet? He's a little cub, naïve, but not a thief; neither is my grandson'

'Sir Charles, Owen Cambridge is back at the station being looked after by my retired father, Brutus. Don't worry—Oliver, Victoria and Thomas are there, too. But PC Rex found one sack of stolen meat in Owen's bedroom,' says a more reflective Sergeant Ali.

'Just like now. Look what I have found under Charlie's bed,' proclaims a proud PC Rex, who is standing at the top of the staircase, holding a full black sack.

'No, it's a set-up. I am innocent. Please believe me,' pleads Charlie.

Charles hangs his head in shame, yet something in the back of his clever mind doesn't add up.

8

The Lazy Chester Brown and Charlie and Owen go to Court

'This is a job you can do, Chester. Foxham Town Hall is looking for a full-time tax inspector. The interviews start tomorrow,' suggests Trudi to Chester, the long-time resident of Foxham Care Home for Foxes.

...

Chester Brown from Ipswich was swept out to sea when he and his fellow farmhands from Ipswich—two foxes including Chester, two dogs and three humans—visited Great Yarmouth one summer's day. After a splendid fish and chips lunch, Chester decided to explore the pier on his own. This was not unusual for Chester, as he had recently taken up photography, and wanted to capture the sea and the sand on this sunny day by himself and with no distractions. Yet, as Chester was pointing his camera's lens at a seagull flying above his head, he slipped on the wet wood and plummeted into the sea. As Chester splashed into the cold water, a huge wave came out of nowhere and took the frightened fox into the unforgiving and brutal North Sea.

Chester, believing his time was up, wept as he passed out, thinking the next time he woke he would be entering Heaven, as Chester, all his life, had been a well behaved and caring fox—maybe a bit lazy, but with no malice whatsoever in his soul.

On the very same Sunday, Trudi, along with her grandmother Anna, was walking along the seafront at Great Yarmouth after eating a fabulous Sunday lunch of roast chicken. Suddenly, Trudi felt a strange sensation that a fellow fox was in trouble. Trudi's intuition made her look out into the North Sea, where she saw a skinny and tall fox, in a waistcoat and shorts, floating on his back, as the sun beamed on the unconscious fox's face.

Trudi, brave as she is, rushed into the sea to save the doomed fox, as unlike most foxes, Trudi has no fear of water, whilst Anna, like her granddaughter, acted quickly and ran to find the coastguard.

The coastguard, Gabriel, a French wolf, had escaped Nazi-occupied France when, as a cub, he and his family swam the English Channel in 1942. Hailed as heroes by the English, Gabriel found that he loved the English seaside, from the sticks of rock to the donkey rides, and decided to dedicate his life to working on the seafront. As well as being the coastguard, he gave—and still does—swimming lessons to the local schools in Great Yarmouth. Gabriel is a respected member of the community.

Within one minute, Gabriel, being cheered on by all the human and animal folk, was in the sea with Trudi and Chester, as he helped Trudi to bring the half-drowned fox to the safety of the beach.

Gabriel wasted no time in giving Chester the kiss of life as he laid on his back on the beach, soaked from the salty sea. Soon, Chester started to cough and regain consciousness. The whole of the beach erupted into euphoria when they saw that the drowned fox was alive. Gabriel was lifted by a few foxes and humans and carried out on to the promenade, as they celebrated what a hero he was—overlooking how brave Trudi had been, much to her annoyance.

After giving Chester a change of clothing, as a bystander had brought a spare pair of shorts and a shirt, Anna, in her red Morris Minor, drove Trudi, still in her wet clothes, and Chester back to Foxham. Chester was admitted straight away into the care home, shaken and with no memory of who he was.

His close and caring friends from Ipswich didn't see the commotion with Chester foolishly falling into the sea. Instead, they went in good faith to the funfair, believing that Chester had sneaked there to have a ride on the merry-go-round. But after an hour of not finding their friend, they reported Chester Brown as a missing fox. However, the Great Yarmouth police failed to see the connection between a fox saved from drowning earlier and the sudden disappearance of a fox.

At first, Chester was simply called Yarmouth by Trudi and the rest of Foxham, as this was the place where she had rescued him from drowning. But within three months, Chester's memory returned, and he wrote to his friends at the farm in Ipswich to tell them that he was safe. They wasted no time in coming to visit their friend and telling him that he had a job and a home with loving friends waiting for him. Chester, truly touched by their generosity, stated he would, but his left leg was seriously damaged and had trouble walking, which then was the truth. Trudi said to the farmhands from Ipswich that she would allow Chester to stay until his leg got better. That was two years ago.

Chester's left leg got better within nine months, but he remembered the farm, the hard work and the long hours, and that during peak season, he and his friends often worked six days a week. At the care home, Chester was very happy and he didn't want to leave, because he had the best room, with a bathroom ensuite, that looked out onto Foxham Woods. He slept in a big warm bed and ate three hot meals a day cooked by Trudi and Anna. All his washing and cleaning was done again by the grandmother and granddaughter, and none of this cost Chester a penny—even though he had a lot of money in a savings account, as his faithful friends would have a whip-round once a month and send him a postal order, as they still believed Chester had a bad left leg.

■ ■ ■

Chester gulps when he hears Trudi mention the word 'job', so in an attempt to defer her from finding him employment, Chester grabs his right leg and starts to cry out in pain (Chester often forgets which leg is meant to be the bad one). Trudi worked out a long time ago that Chester was fit for work, yet over the past two years, Trudi and Chester have become best friends, so, Trudi doesn't want to turf him out.

Trudi doesn't mind if Chester doesn't want to return to the farm; she just wants him to pay his own way in life. Chester's permanent residency at the Fox's care home is costing them a lot of money from the funds that are raised from jumble sales, sponsored walks and such like, which are topped up by generous annual donations from the likes of Charles Renard and other wealthy foxes. But this money is meant to help foxes in need, not a 'freeloader' like Chester.

Even though Chester is not a wicked fox, he is selfish and foolish.

At the start of this summer, Chester bought a bright red bicycle from his savings that he rides around Foxham Woods away from the village, believing no one will see him. Chester hides the bike underneath the leaves and branches in the wood, when he is not riding it. Yet Trudi, like Anna, has seen him riding his bike, but not said a word.

Chester, a keen photographer before his accident at Great Yarmouth, unfortunately lost his camera in the sea. So, last year, his friends from Ipswich bought him a camera and a brown satchel for him to carry it in because Trudi had written to them out of despair, stating that all Chester does is listen to the radio and read comics. So, his caring friends helped to rekindle Chester's interest in photography. Trudi turned the basement in the care home into a dark room, for Chester to develop his photos.

Chester is a talented photographer. Trudi and many others are amazed by how beautiful and captivating his photos of the folks and sights of Foxham are—so much so that Victoria Cambridge, the mother of Thomas and Owen and editor of *The Foxham Gazette*, offered Chester a job as a photographer, although again Chester grabbed whatever leg and started to cry.

∎ ∎ ∎

'Chester, you have got to find a job and stop acting like a cub. Okay, you don't want to work on the farm, but you foolishly turned down the chance to be a photographer for *The Foxham Gazette* and Victoria won't give you a second chance. This job, you can do, and I will march you to the interview. Foxham is growing and we need to make sure everyone pays their taxes, unlike that rascal Ferdy,' declares a now flustered Trudi.

Chester, sensing Trudi's anger, believes limping off with his head down will make her feel sorry for him and shut her up. It is a tactic that he has used many times, yet Chester has never realised that Trudi was just going along with him. Today, Trudi Milanese has had enough.

'No, Chester, that won't work any more. I have known for some time that your leg is fine. I believe that you are a good and honest fox, not a scoundrel like Ferdy. He and his son, Charlie, have brought nothing but shame to the good name of the Renards. Charlie is a wicked little cub, and a bad influence on Owen, who is such a sweet cub. I know it broke Victoria's heart when she had to write the headline and copy for *The Foxham Gazette* the other day that her own son Owen, along with that rogue Charlie, have been charged with stealing meat from Blades the butcher,' says a reflective yet angry Trudi.

Chester, who is good friends with Charlie and Owen, hangs his head in shame. Trudi, with her psychic ability, even though she still doesn't know she is a good witch, senses something is troubling her friend. 'Chester is there something you want to tell me?' Trudi demands.

Chester, knowing that his friend is not going to let him limp off to his room, looks at Trudi with sad eyes then cries out, 'They didn't do it. It was Penelope Painshill, Blades the butcher and PC Rex who paid Mrs Duke to say she saw Owen and Charlie steal the meat.'

Trudi, knowing that Chester is telling the truth, faints on the spot.

■ ■ ■

The crowd outside Foxham Magistrates Court is gathering and getting tetchy, as the recent theft of the meat from Blades the butcher has sadly divided this usually harmonious village in Norfolk.

Reggie Collins, a human pensioner and widower, loves his sausages and every Friday morning goes to Blades to purchase them for the weekend, as he has sausages and chips for his Friday dinner, two sausage sandwiches for his breakfast on Saturday, toad-in-the-hole for his lunch, sausage and mash for his dinner, sausage with a fried egg for his breakfast on Sunday, sausage and baked beans for his Sunday lunch, then all the remaining sausages are used for his famous sausage casserole for dinner, which is washed down with a few bottles of brown ale.

However, when Blades told him that his beloved sausages had been stolen and he wouldn't get any more until the following week, Reggie wept more than he did at his wife's funeral. So, when the news quickly spread that Charlie Renard and Owen Cambridge were the culprits, Reggie went berserk and went round to Fox Hill Hall to show his anger, only to be punched on the nose by Boris.

Reggie didn't press charges but that was the fateful day that the conflict in Foxham began. Many folks in Foxham, from foxes to humans, liked Reggie, so they sided with him, believing that Charlie and Owen should be given 10 years hard labour. But some of the folk sided with the Renards and the Cambridges, believing that the two cubs were innocent. Fights and arguments were now the norm in Foxham over the theft, which breaks Trudi's heart in seeing how divided the village is.

The frightened Charlie and Owen, under the police escort of Sergeant Ali, PC Bryan and PC Rex, arrive at Foxham Magistrates Court in a beaten up 'meat wagon' from Foxham police station. It is a pleasant 10-minute walk, but the magistrate Penelope Painshill insisted that the two cubs were to be transported like convicts, in order to bring shame to them and their families.

For the past two weeks, Charlie and Owen have been incarcerated at the police station, mainly for their own safety. The retired Sergeant Brutus, now the police station's caretaker and sometimes the jailer, built the two cubs a nice bunk bed, laid down a carpet, bought them comics, and cooked them a nice meal every evening. He allowed their families to visit them whenever they wanted, put a wireless in the cell, and he even kept the cell open, so Charlie and Owen could wander about. And with it being summer, Brutus would escort the young prisoners to Foxham Common for a kick about and some tree climbing, which incensed people like Reggie, who would shout out, 'Hang them,' as he walked past in disgust.

■ ■ ■

'You little xxxxs! Hang the xxxx, xxxx,' screams Reggie and his supporters, with language so foul that I daren't repeat it, dear readers. Trembling and terrified, the two cubs, shackled and dressed in striped prison outfits like those of a chain gang, step out of the van to face the crowd. Charlie and Owen's attire were the instructions of Penelope Painshill—she relishes humiliating people.

'Say goodbye to your families. You won't be seeing them for a while and where you are going, there ain't no such thing as Christmas. I will be thinking of you two when I am tucking into my turkey on Christmas Day. Why, there's a young man that goes by the name of Bernie Matthews, who is breeding and selling turkeys nearby and they are bootiful!' says a happy PC Rex, who doesn't see Bernard Matthews standing directly behind him.

The young Bernard Matthews doesn't appreciate how these cubs are being treated, yet he likes the term 'bootiful' to describe his poultry.

Despite the cruel attempt by PC Rex to break the spirit of Charlie and Owen, the shackled cubs are given some hope when they hear loud shouts of 'Free the Foxham Two' and 'They are innocent', as they climb up the stone steps of the court.

When Charlie and Owen, being led by PC Rex, get to the top of the grey stone steps, Charlie turns around, looks at the folks gazing at him and the village in the background, then starts to cry. 'Don't cry,' says Oliver, who along with his family and Charles and his family is at the entrance of the court to meet and support Charlie and Owen.

Ferdy, who was arrested the same day as Charlie, is also here not as a defendant but as a spectator. Ferdy was only kept in the cells overnight and fined the following morning by the magistrate Penelope Painshill—20 shillings for disturbing the peace; the charge of trying to bribe a police officer was dropped. Ferdy yawned and pulled the money out of his chino trousers—and was fined a further 20 shillings for contempt of court by Penelope Painshill, for she detests the Renard family.

▪ ▪ ▪

When Penelope Painshill and her family moved to Foxham from Cobham Surrey to start work as the magistrate, she believed, due to her and her husband's ancestry, that she should, by right, be the leader of Foxham and all foxes in Europe.

For, you see, Penelope comes from a family of foxes that sided with the squires that hunted the wood foxes, and Penelope thinks that foxes that descend from the woods do not deserve the luxuries that she was born into. Yet Penelope Painshill has never been told that her great-great-grandmother June D'abernons started off as a washer fox for the squire of Esher. June D'abernons was cunning and it didn't take her long before she conned her way to becoming the right-hand fox to the squire, but June's rise is another story all together.

In nearby Cobham, as June D'abernons was social climbing in Esher, Victor Painshill, a young fox who was a carpenter by trade, was working his charm with the elite humans. For his great-great-grandson is none other than Sebastian Painshill, Penelope's husband. Sebastian is a happy-go-lucky fox; however, his wife Penelope is just as cunning as her great-great-grandmother and will play any trick she can to get to the top. So, for Penelope, Charles Renard is standing in her way.

But Penelope Painshill knows that Charles is a clever fox and probably would outsmart her in a debate. Consequently, she has decided to frame his grandson and to expose his son Ferdy as a tax evader, as it was she who created the role of a tax inspector at Foxham Town Hall just to investigate Ferdy. Penelope trusts that with both Charlie and Ferdy charged and sentenced, the village of Foxham will lose its trust in the family name and she will step up to be the new leader of this community.

In order to frame Charlie, Penelope Painshill requested for PC Rex to be stationed at Foxham, for his corruption and brutal methods are adored and celebrated by the police, magistrates and judges across Great Britain. Penelope believes that getting Ferdy will be easier, as he hasn't paid taxes since 1939, and it's now 1957—that's just under 20 years of him evading the Inland Revenue.

Penelope Painshill has other ruthless intents that go beyond being a community leader. She wants to turn Foxham Care Home for Foxes into luxury flats and Milano's into an exclusive restaurant. Penelope Painshill plans to raise the cost of living across Foxham, so all the hard-working humans, foxes, dogs and badgers are forced to leave, turning the village into an exclusive residential area for the rich, as Penelope hates the working class, especially the foxes.

Her husband Sebastian, who enjoys living in the village, is oblivious to her cunning plan. Her daughter Isabella loves Foxham—she even asked to join The Young Rascals, only to be told by Charlie that no girls are allowed. Her son Henry, who doesn't know that his mother is scheming, is starting to warm to Foxham. So, all three are happy with the way things are, but Penelope certainly isn't.

■ ■ ■

'Charlie, be brave,' says his grandfather Charles to his grandson, as he and Owen enter the Magistrates Court.

By Charles' side is Arnold Layton Strong, the first fox defence lawyer, who possesses an excellent success rate. Arnold, who usually works at and socialises around the Old Bailey before returning to his home in Hampstead, did not hesitate for one second when Charles telephoned him, asking if he could represent his grandson and his friend Owen. Charles said to Oliver Cambridge, Owen's father, that he would cover the barrister's fee and Oliver would never be in debt to him.

Arnold and Charles have been friends for years. Arnold remembers when Charles started as a junior at the Bank of England and he was an office cub at a law firm around the corner. They both rented bedsits in Hackney, and would catch the same Tube to the City and have lunch together—chicken sandwiches at a nearby Italian deli. After work, they both would jump on the Tube back to Hackney. Then, in the evening, Arnold and Charles would visit the local taverns or pie and mash shop, before retiring back to their cosy and homely bedsits—good times for these then-ambitious young and handsome foxes.

Arnold offered his services for nothing, but Charles insisted on paying, as he knows Arnold had a wife and three cubs' mouths to feed.

'Yes, grandfather,' weeps Charlie.

'Charlie, please trust me. You and your friend Owen will walk free,' states Arnold.

Charlie looks at the dapper Arnold in a three-piece blue suit, with a gold watch and chain on the waistcoat. Arnold's demeanour and words briefly reassure Charlie, just before he and Owen are brutally dragged away by PC Rex.

Then PC Rex is stopped in his tracks by Sergeant Ali: 'PC Rex, I will escort the prisoners into the court. You go and see to the crowd.'

'Yes, sarg,' whimpers PC Rex.

9

The Trial of Charlie and Owen

'Wake up, Trudi! Wake up!' says a concerned Chester, as he breaks open a bottle of smelling salts under his friend's nose, from the first aid box. The odour from the contents of the bottle is so strong that Trudi leaps up from the first whiff.

The now-standing Trudi looks at Chester and says, 'Thank you and now we have to save Charlie and Owen. Okay, Charlie is rude and annoying, but he might grow out of it, although his father Ferdy is no better—the apple certainly hasn't fallen far from the tree. But little Owen is so sweet and innocent.'

Chester giggles a little, as he has witnessed Owen egging Charlie on to do mischief in Foxham. Yet the common belief in the village is that Charlie is leading Owen astray, which pleases Owen no end.

'This is no laughing matter, Chester Brown. Silly me, I am a silly fox sometimes…'

Chester, who gets cheeky when he is worried, foolishly cuts Trudi off in midsentence. 'I am pleased you admit to being silly, as I have been meaning to tell you for some time now.'

'Don't be rude, Chester. I am a silly fox because I fainted before I could ask you how you know that Penelope Painshill is in cahoots with PC Rex and Blades the butcher… wipe that smirk off your face. Well, how do you know?' retorts Trudi so loudly that she wakes up all the resting and genuinely ill foxes in the care home.

Chester, feeling the full wrath of Trudi, meekly starts to recall the day he witnessed this unholy trio hatching their diabolical plan.

'I went out on my red bike…' Chester pauses, as he knows he has just admitted to Trudi that his left leg is fine.

'Chester, I know about the bike, but what you are declaring is serious, so I am giving you amnesty over your left leg. And before you ask, it means I don't care that you have been lying about your left leg… So, Chester: please continue.'

Chester, relieved that Trudi won't punish him over his deception, carries on with his recollection. 'Thank you, Trudi. So, I went into Foxham Woods, propped my bike against a tree and took my camera out of the satchel. It was such a lovely day—blue skies and all that—so naturally, I started to take photos. Then I smelt a barbeque nearby, and I know that Charles Renard and Sergeant Ali have banned them in the woods. So, I followed the smell of cooking, and saw PC Rex, Blades the butcher and Mrs Painshill in an opening amongst the trees.'

'Very clever—cooking and eating the evidence,' states an intrigued Trudi.

'Yes, it was cos I heard PC Rex say, "This is the meat that those little urchins, Charlie and Owen, stole. Bootiful!" All three started to laugh, just like villains I've seen at the pictures. Even though I was scared, I hid behind a tree and took a few photos. You know, just in case.'

'Good thinking, Chester,' praises Trudi.

'I heard Mrs Painshill say, "PC Rex, when you search those little toerags' houses, have a black sack in your tunic pocket and make sure you go into their bedrooms alone then fill it with toys and books. No one is going to question the honest paw of the law," which was followed by more evil laughter. Then Blades the butcher, who was doing the cooking, said, "You should have seen old Reggie Collins' face when I told him that his sausages had been nicked—he cried like a baby." All three started to laugh like villains again.'

'I get the gist about the laughter,' says Trudi, longing for Chester to complete his yarn.

'I was painting you the picture. Anyhow, Mrs Painshill looked at some notes in a file, closed it, and said, "You'll get a nice insurance pay-out, Blades—enough for that new home you want and a day trip to Great Yarmouth. PC Rex, I will say Sergeant Ali is incompetent, so you'll be promoted, with a nice pay rise." To which PC Rex replied, "Bootiful!" Then they… oh, sorry, I won't mention them laughing again. After they stopped, well, you know, Mrs Painshill said, "With Charlie going to prison and Charles' son Ferdy being investigated by the taxman, this is enough for the folk around here to say he is unfit to rule and I will take over. PC Rex, make sure Mrs Duke sticks to the story when she testifies in court. Then she will go on a long holiday, never to return."'

'Then more evil laughter?' adds Trudi.

'How did you know?' asks a surprised Chester.

'Just a hunch,' smirks Trudi.

'After hearing this and taking enough photos, I put the camera in me satchel and ride off to tell you, Trudi, of their evil plan. But whether nerves or whatever, I fall off me bike. The landing must have startled them, as all three run over to see me on my back, with my bike on top of me. A furious PC Rex says he will arrest me for fraud, as I am fit, and been living here under deception. The nasty Mrs Painshill says she will send me to prison for six years, where foxes like me will be bullied by the prisoners and guards every day, and then the brute Blades says when I get released, he will kidnap me and turn me into mincemeat if I ever say what I saw. So please, Trudi, I can't say a word. Please don't make me.'

Trudi, outraged by how cruel the three have been to Chester and wicked to Charlie and Owen, firmly asks, 'Chester, did they take your camera and satchel?'

'No, it's safely in my bedroom, and I developed the photos last night, as I see there's a competition in Norwich for the best wildlife photography.'

Trudi jumps for joy, then says, 'Chester, fetch your photos. There are two innocent foxes that need saving. Stand up to these bullies and you will be a hero forever in Foxham. I will give you the job as the caretaker and you can keep your room. You love this home, so looking after it will be second nature. Chester, you are a good and kind fox, and today you have to be a courageous one.'

Chester, inspired by her words, puffs his chest out and replies, 'I will get my photos. My red bike is in the woods.'

'I know where it is; I even put a lock on it in the evening.'

'Thank you. Come on: let's ride to Foxham Court and save our friends, Charlie and Owen.'

'Bravo,' yells Trudi.

■ ■ ■

'Charlie Jasper Renard, how do you plead?' asks Penelope Painshill.

'Not guilty,' pleads Charlie.

'You lying little xxxx. Hang him!' screams Reggie Collins from the public gallery, that looks down onto the court.

'Mr Collins, I do appreciate that you are annoyed, but one more outburst like that and I will have no choice but to charge you with contempt of court. Do I make myself clear?' commands Penelope Painshill.

'Yes and sorry your honour. It's just I ain't got no bangers for me dinner,' sobs a genuinely heartbroken Reggie.

Then PC Rex, who has been given the task of keeping order in the public gallery, gives Reggie a quick yet powerful jab to his jaw. The surprise and pain of the punch shakes Reggie, who is suddenly overwhelmed with fear, sensing something isn't right.

'Owen Geoffrey Cambridge, how do you plead?'

Trembling due to the sheer terror of the occasion, Owen looks over his left shoulder and up to his parents and older brother Thomas in the public gallery, turns back to Penelope Painshill, and screams out, 'It's a lie, I never stole from Blades. Please believe me.'

'Master Cambridge, one more emotional outburst like that and I will impose a long sentence upon you without a hearing. It is within my power,' snaps the heartless Penelope Painshill.

'Objection,' bellows a confident Arnold Layton Strong. 'Master Cambridge is anxious and upset, due to the charge. Of which I will prove that he, along with Master Renard, are innocent and they are fearful due to this trial and public spectacle. This is a lot for two young, loving and caring foxes to handle.' Arnold, in his wig and gown, turns to the jury of two female foxes, three male foxes, three women, two men and two badgers, male and female, and takes a bow, which is met by some applause.

Penelope Painshill had written to the Home Office stating that, due to what she thought was the magnitude of the crime, a jury would be required—and the Home Office agreed. For Penelope Painshill believes that the incriminating evidence; the oath of PC Rex, who found the sacks of meat in their bedrooms, yet he had to dispose of the meat for health and safety reasons; and the eyewitness account of Mrs Duke are enough to find Charlie and Owen guilty without any reasonable doubt. Therefore, no one would suspect that the crime and trial is a fraud. Hence, Penelope Painshill's request for a jury, so this travesty of justice will seem authentic.

'Your honour, I see that my learned friend Mr Strong is taking this opportunity to practise his rather amateur acting skills,' snaps Gerald Viper for the prosecution. A Siberian Husky with a severe reputation for grilling suspects on the stand, he is so harsh that many have changed their plea from not guilty to guilty due to his onslaught of questions during a trial.

'Objection overruled. Well observed, Mr Viper. Mr Strong, this is not a game of charades with your family during the festive holiday. No, sir, this is a trial, where a serious crime—that of theft—has been committed. And if one of the accused is too emotional to make a simple plea of guilty or not guilty then I will deem that he is refusing to stand trial and declare a verdict of guilty,' retorts the honourable Penelope Painshill, nodding to Gerald Viper, who gleefully smiles as he sits down. Viper by name, viper by nature.

Arnold Layton Strong, accustomed to aggressive judges and prosecution law-yers, turns to face Penelope Painshill. 'Thank you, your honour. Yet you cannot declare the accused guilty, the same as you cannot declare him not guilty due to his anxiety.'

'Excellent point,' shouts out Charles from the public gallery, which is met with a few hums of approval in the court—much to the delight of those supporting Charlie and Owen.

'Mr Strong, I know you are an experienced and intelligent lawyer. Your reputa-tion from the Old Bailey precedes you. Yet may I remind you—one more remark like that then I will view that as insubordination and have you removed from my court. Do I make myself clear?' says Penelope Painshill in a sinister manner, making some of the folk in the court gasp at her powerful declaration.

Arnold adjusts his wig, puts both of his paws on the lapels of his gown, and walks forward to Penelope Painshill's bench. 'Yes, your honour, yet you will find that I can question you, your actions and your opinions. We thankfully beat an op-pressive regime, in favour of freedom, and that includes the freedom of speech and thought.'

Penelope Painshill glares at the now rather smug Arnold Layton Strong, as she replies. 'A fair point, even though delivered in a melodramatic manner. Now back to the hearing. Owen Geoffrey Cambridge, how do you plead? Guilty or not guilty.'

Owen, now feeling stimulated by the bravery of Arnold Layton Strong, faces Penelope Painshill and fearlessly declares, 'Not guilty.'

'Bravo,' yells out Thomas, in support of his brother.

Penelope Painshill, wishing to proceed with her cunning plan, decides not to warn Thomas that he could be held in contempt of court. Otherwise, that may entail another monologue from Arnold Layton Strong, who outside of the world of law, is a member of the Hampstead amateur dramatic society.

'Your pleas have been accepted, and as both of you have pleaded not guilty, I call this court to order, and for the trial to commence. Call the first witness for the prosecution,' orders Penelope Painshill, who is hoping to have Charlie and Owen sentenced by teatime.

'Call the first witness: Mrs Joan Duke,' orders the court usher, Otto Farsund, a young fox from Norway, who found himself in Foxham, after coming in from a ship that docked at Cromer, Norfolk, from Oslo.

Otto had been offered a job as a trainee accountant at Norwich City Football Club via Vålerenga FC on an exchange programme. Yet Otto rather foolishly lost his money, passport and letter with a job offer. With only enough money to catch the bus to Foxham, Otto thought he would find sanctuary in this famous village for foxes.

But when he went to the town hall to seek their help, Otto was interviewed by none other than Penelope Painshill, who at the time needed an admin clerk and a court usher. Otto, sadly for him, was bullied into this role, as Penelope said he could go to prison for five years for being an illegal fox with no papers unless he took the job. However, all is not lost, as his father is getting him a new passport, and chasing Norwich City Football Club for a copy of the letter that offered his son a job.

■ ■ ■

'Be still, Chester. Five more minutes and we will be at the court,' says the bossy Trudi, riding Chester's red bike, as he sits on the crossbar.

■ ■ ■

'Mrs Duke, can you point to which of these young foxes said they would duff you up if you told the police?' asks Gerald Viper.

'Him, the 'orrible looking one, with those evil eyes,' says Mrs Duke as she points to a confused Charlie, before bringing her hands to her face, as she pretends to cry.

'No further questions. Your honour, may I suggest no questions from my learned friend, as it is clear that Mrs Duke is too stressed to answer them,' suggests Gerald Viper in a sly manner.

'Objection, it is the duty of the court to allow the defence to question the witness. This is a travesty of justice,' protests Arnold.

'Objection overruled. The witness has suffered a severe shock and her bravery in the witness box has only heightened the trauma. What you are asking goes against the Geneva Convention. No, I say that Mrs Duke is to leave this court, get a taxi to Norwich train station, catch the next train to Great Yarmouth, and spend a weekend there. The court will cover the costs. Otto, please go and get the petty cash and give all of it to Mrs Duke,' orders Penelope Painshill, who is now drunk on power.

'Your honour, the rules of the Geneva Convention apply to war and war alone. I insist that you allow me to question Mrs Duke, or I will declare that you are biased and unfit to judge this trial. Please remember I have witnesses.'

'PC Rex, did you hear Mr Arnold just threaten me in a whisper, after he said, "I have witnesses"?' asks Penelope Painshill, knowing full well what the answer will be.

'Yes, I did, your honour,' confirms PC Rex, who has come down from the public gallery to the court, for he is to be the next witness.

'Very well. PC Rex, please arrest Mr Arnold, take him to the police station and charge him with threatening behaviour. Master Renard and Master Cambridge, you will have to defend yourselves,' says Penelope Painshill, believing this ruse will stack the odds very much in her favour.

'You are not arresting anyone, PC Rex, and you, Mrs Painshill, are a traitor,' yells Trudi. The whole court gasps, as she and the nervous Chester make their way to the bench, clutching the implicating photos.

'Trudi Milanese, you are nothing more than a common cook and carer. How dare you enter my court in such a threatening and rude manner, along with the laziest fox to ever walk this earth? PC Rex, PC Bryan and Sergeant Ali, arrest these nasty foxes at once,' demands Penelope Painshill, feeling uneasy for she is aware that Chester knows the truth.

Yet Sergeant Ali, the police dog who loves and adores the community of Foxham, knows that Trudi, the well behaved and caring fox, and Chester, the fox who just wants a quiet life, would not disrupt this court case without a good reason.

'Your honour, as the chief upholder of law and order in Foxham, I overrule your order. I am going to allow Ms Milanese and Mr Brown, to have their say,' says a confident Sergeant Ali.

'I will see that you and your father hang from the gallows. This is my court and what I say goes,' screams an anxious Penelope Painshill, as PC Rex nervously pulls down the collar of his white shirt, thinking that the game might be up.

'No, it is the court for the folk of Foxham and your role is to see that justice is served by the letter of the law. You cannot hang two upstanding dogs of this community, just because you don't like what Sergeant Ali said,' remarks Charles, from the public gallery as he reclaims his role as the leader of Foxham. Arnold Layton Strong looks up and nods at his friend.

'I will burn you at the stake, along with your son and grandson,' shrieks Penelope Painshill, who is getting more scared by the second.

Trudi, sensing that this argument is likely to go on all day, decides to take control of the situation, as she so often does. Consequently, the young brave vixen jumps on the dark oak and grand court desk, which Arnold is standing next to, and holds up a handful of photos. 'Here, thanks to Chester, I have proof that Blades, PC Rex and Penelope Painshill were scheming in Foxham Woods. And, like all villains, their vanity is their downfall. As you can see in these photos, Penelope Painshill is holding a folder, with the words "Framing Charlie Renard and Owen Cambridge for stealing meat from Blades".'

'And look! Blades is cooking 24 sausages and 10 steaks, and next to the barbeque is a lot of mince, and some ham and pork. This is the meat that was reported stolen. It was PC Rex who found the sacks in Charlie and Owen's bedrooms, which he filled with their books and toys, as he knew no one would question his evidence,' declares a now very brave Chester.

The whole court, apart from Trudi, Chester, Penelope Painshill, PC Rex, Mrs Duke and Blades the butcher, gasp in astonishment.

'I told you we should have got rid of that idiot Chester. I xxxx told you,' screams Blades the butcher, as he makes a run for the court exit, only to be rugby-tackled by Thomas, who came down from the public gallery the moment he saw Trudi and Chester enter the court.

'Off with their heads,' yells the bemused Penelope Painshill, thinking she is the Queen of Hearts from *Alice's Adventures in Wonderland*.

'Sergeant Ali and PC Bryan, arrest her, PC Rex, Blades the butcher and Mrs Duke,' orders Charles, whose words are greeted by loud applause and cheers.

'Release the prisoners. They are free to go without a stain on their characters,' declares Arnold Layton Strong. Gerald Viper nods with approval, for he genuinely thought Charlie and Owen were guilty, as he had been misled by Penelope Painshill and PC Rex.

Charlie and Owen, still in their shackles, jump for joy, just like when they hear that Norwich City has won a football game.

■ ■ ■

Due to all the excitement, Trudi and Chester have both decided to stay in the court as it clears out, and as it does, a pleased Trudi says to her friend, 'You were very brave today, Chester Brown. You saved two innocent foxes; you can walk about Foxham with your head held high.'

Chester smiles, gets up and walks out into the sunshine to enjoy the rest of the day with a bike ride. But as he gets out of the court, he sees Charlie riding his red bike with Owen on the crossbar, still in their prison outfits.

'Good scam of yours, Owen, to steal Chester's bike.'

'Yeah, no one will believe Chester, as the whole of Foxham now think we are two sweet innocent foxes.'

Charlie and Owen both start to laugh like villains from a film.

10

The Departure

Mario Bandito, along with the entourage of his close family, employees and new-found friends, arrives back at his sea-view apartment at Viale Anton Dohrn on Boxing Day evening, after spending an extraordinary yet pleasurable Christmas Day with the kind-hearted and fearless folk of Sant'Agata de' Goti.

Mario's luxury apartment was the one-time home of his boss, Vittorio Mosele, who was reported missing after he vanished on a fishing trip in the Bay of Naples a few years back with Mario. The finger of suspicion quietly but firmly points at Mario over Mosele's disappearance, yet no one in Naples dares breathe a word that Mario may be behind the powerful crime boss' vanishing.

Upon arrival at the apartment, Silvia, Mario's strong-minded wife and Alberto's loving mother, ushers all but the immediate family and friends into the street, whilst she, along with their live-in cook Sophia, a human, prepare a huge dish of parmigiana di melanzane, as the Bandito's traditional Italian kitchen always has plenty of aubergines, mozzarella and tomatoes hanging from the dark oak beams.

As Silvia, a passionate cook, and Sophia are busy cooking, Carlotta keeps Alberto occupied by showing him the latest rock 'n' roll dances in the living room; otherwise, the young fox would eat all the ingredients before anyone else is fed. Meanwhile, Diabolo decides to take his gang, the boxing wolf brothers from Benevento, Leonardo and Francesco, and the bears of Campania into the street that looks out onto the sea for a nice and relaxing late-night supper.

'Your troops, the two wolves and the bears, can't know the real reason for your departure to Foxham, as it will be worrying them no end. Say it is a sabbatical for Alberto to recover from his recent abduction and they are to remain here to fight

off the evil forces. Don Mario, make sure this evening that no one gets drunk, as we need to keep our wits about us,' says Carlotta to Mario, as he pours himself a ginger ale in his splendid living room, whilst Alberto is trying to do the bunny hop dance.

'Wise words,' agrees Mario, as he sits down on his brown leather Chesterfield-style sofa, clutching a crystal glass tumbler in his right paw.

'Mario, we need to leave Naples tonight after dinner. We are not safe here. We will not be safe until Trudi Milanese can lift the curse on Alberto on Easter Sunday in Foxham,' says a concerned Carlotta, who is standing before the fox crime boss.

Mario gazes up at the beautiful good witch and says, 'Why can't I unite with all my rivals and, after dinner, we go and burn down Castello e Torre di Montesarchio, with all the witches in it?'

'I told you that the castle is protected and anyway, fire won't lift the curse from Alberto. Mario, I am sorry to say that your usual "brutal approach" to business won't beat the witches and their allies,' retorts Carlotta.

Silvia, upon hearing the conversation between Mario and Carlotta, comes out of the kitchen and wearily says, 'We will have to go tomorrow morning as the airport is closed.' Silvia, a lover of the festive period since she was a cub, had not envisaged spending Christmas night in a two-star guest house with a shared bathroom in Sant'Agata de' Goti. Even though Silvia found the folk of the village very loving, she believes their standards in terms of food and living conditions are below hers. Nonetheless, Silvia is a snob, but she will never admit that she is.

'After dinner, I am going to play Snakes and Ladders with Alberto, while eating a slice of panettone and sipping a nice glass of dry spumante. Then a hot bath before a good night's sleep in my own bed. What about our good friend, Stefano Romano? He can fly us, can't he?' asks Silvia.

'I am not asking him, as he will be spending Christmas with his wife and two daughters,' snaps Mario.

'No need to take that tone, Mario. Okay, we can get first-class airline tickets tomorrow. I know Luigi (a fox) well at the Alitalia desk—his father and my father were good friends. He will give us a good price, so no more talk of witches and curses. Alberto, go and fetch the silver cake case from under my bed; in the case, you will find the panettone,' declares Silvia.

Alberto hangs his head in shame, as he had already found the panettone in the silver cake case and ate it on the evening he was kidnapped by Ettore the black cat, Andriana, Benedetta and Caterina. Silvia knows the shamefaced look of her son only too well.

'Alberto Bandito, yes, you should feel disgraced. Every Christmas and Easter it is the same—you eat all the cakes and chocolate. That's it, tomorrow, we will drive down to Calais and I will enlist you in the French Foreign Legion,' screams a now annoyed Silvia.

As Silvia's voice booms out of the apartment and onto the street below, Diabolo and his entourage snigger in between bites of the tasty parmigiana di melanzane.

'Madame Silvia, I do appreciate your concerns and annoyance over Alberto, but we must leave tonight. The witches and the red-cap goblins will regroup and seek revenge. Diana will call out to all the ghouls and other evils that lurk in the forests, lanes, empty castles and graveyards to attack us. For she, on this Earth, is the leader of all things that are evil, whilst Alberto is the saviour of all things that are good. Despite his love for fine food, Alberto has a good and pure heart… No. Don't. I know what you are going to say: "No one tells me what to do." Madame Silvia, not only is your son in danger but so is the rest of the world,' says the ever-strong minded Carlotta.

Silvia, relishing an argument, steps forward to face Carlotta. But Alberto steps in between his loving mother and new best friend, and says, 'Mamma, Carlotta, please don't argue. If we must go tonight, then we must go. But how will we get out of Naples? We can't fly and Diana with her army will be watching the roads.'

'By boat,' suggests Mario.

'A luxury cruise to England would be delightful. Sophia, go and pack my best clothes,' says a now excited Silvia, who loves to travel by boat. Silvia and many other foxes started to lose their fear of water after the war, as they soon found out that travelling by water, be it the sea or a lake, is good fun.

'Madame Silvia, we don't have time for a luxury cruise, even though I think it is an excellent idea. We will have to get a fishing trawler to Marseille, then catch a train across France to Calais, then Calais to Dover,' says Carlotta.

'Madame Carlotta, there is no way that I, Silvia Bandito, is going to set foot, let alone sail, in a common fishing boat. I would rather stay and fight the witches,' yells Silvia.

Mario, seeing sense, decides to take control of the situation. 'Silvia, pack an overnight bag. We will have to leave soon, because the sooner we get to England, the sooner we can stop this evil. I saw evil on Christmas Eve and what I do for a living is not evil, but what the witches do is.'

'Yes, it might not be evil, papa, but it's not legal either,' cuts in a newly assured Alberto, who before his kidnapping and possible sacrifice by the witches of Benevento, followed by a miraculous escape with an equally spectacular battle against the witches and red-cap goblins, never doubted his father's career, but now he does.

'Alberto, the food you eat, the roof over your head, the clothes on your back, the best seats at football and the dining at the finest restaurants comes from this thing of ours. Your grandfather, God rest his soul, was a master pickpocket, not because he wanted to steal, but he had to steal to put food on the table. I didn't starve as a cub, but I didn't have the life of luxury that you have now. What do you want me to do? Give all my money away?' bites Mario.

'Well, that could be a start,' says a confident Alberto.

'I would have never spoken to my father like that. Go to the broom cupboard, Alberto. That is where you will sleep tonight,' screams a shocked and equally annoyed Mario.

'Don Mario, this is not the time for punishing Alberto for being rude to you, and Alberto this is not the time to be cheeky to your father. We must leave Naples right at this moment—I can sense evil approaching. Foxham will offer us better protection and lift the curse in April, because if we don't then you, and the rest of the world will never see Christmas Day again,' says Carlotta, taking control of the situation while trying not to offend a mafia boss.

'Madame Carlotta, you speak wise words and your concern for my son is overwhelming. Okay, let's head to the bay, find the first boat,' says Mario, knowing that he and his family are in danger.

'Not a fishing boat,' screams Silvia.

'Silvia, be quiet,' says Mario in a soft voice.

■ ■ ■

'It is a sign from either Heaven or Hell,' declares a cautious Diabolo upon seeing the fishing trawler, Viaqua, docked in the Bay of Santa Lucia, which is usually a pleasant stroll from Mario's apartment. But this evening, Diabolo, Mario, Silvia, Alberto, Carlotta and a small entourage consisting of a handful of foxes and men from Mario's gang, Leonardo and Francesco the two boxing wolves from Benevento, and Giorgio and a few of the bears of Campania, do not appreciate the surrounding beauty, due to the fact that there is the threat of evil in the air.

The rest of Mario's troops and the bears of Campania, along with other 'Neapolitan families', are patrolling the streets and countryside of their beloved city to fend off any attacks from the witches and their allies.

Viaqua was the fishing trawler that Diabolo boarded from Albania a few years back, hoping to see the world. Upon this trawler, Diabolo became good friends with the two wolves, Wilfred and Winston, the bear, Rocco, and the fox, Rossi. As you may remember, the poor Doberman fell into the sea after being chased across the ship's deck by the one-eyed sailor Krojan, who was wielding a sword, as he pursued Diabolo.

'Dear Diabolo, you have often spoken about your loving friends from this ship and those evil men in charge. If these nasty men are still on board then I will not hesitate for a second to seek revenge in your name,' declares Mario to his good friend.

'Thank you, Mario, but it is a sign from Heaven,' cries a now joyous Diabolo as he falls to his knees upon seeing Rossi the fox, who comes out of the trawler's cabin onto the deck, looking dutiful. The whiff of fine cooking comes out of the open ship's door, which makes both Mario's and Alberto's mouths water—even though father and son only finished the last of the parmigiana di melanzane just over an hour ago.

'Rossi, it is I, Diabolo,' shouts out the happy liver-coloured Doberman. Rossi looks back in sheer disbelief and then shouts out with much joy, 'Rocco, it's Diabolo.'

Suddenly, a large brown bear dressed in a thick blue jumper and dark trousers with a dark blue sailor's cap steps onto the deck from the cabin and starts to cry when he sees Diabolo, a friend that Rocco thought had died at sea. Diabolo gets off his knees and runs towards Viaqua as fast as he can.

Carlotta, sensing the genuine love and the chance to sail out of Naples, beckons Silvia and Alberto to follow Diabolo. As Silvia walks past Carlotta, she says: 'Oh my, this will be an adventure.' Carlotta is delighted to see a change of heart from Silvia, who an hour or so ago detested the notion of setting foot upon a fishing trawler.

'Don Mario, instruct your gang to guard us before we sail. I will see you on board,' says Carlotta, to which Mario nods. Even though no one has yet asked if any of the crew of Viaqua don't mind sailing to Marseille, Carlotta—witch or not—just knows they will say yes.

Soon, Rossi, Rocco and Diabolo are hugging on deck like the long-lost friends they are.

Diabolo senses straight away that captain Izet, Koll and his one-eyed brother Krojan are no more. For Diabolo knew in his heart of hearts that a mutiny led by Rocco would be too powerful for the despicable trio to handle. Then the Doberman, nervously asks, 'Where are Wilfred and Winston? Please don't tell me they drowned at sea.'

'No, no, they settled down in Ireland with two Irish female wolves. We used to do fishing trips to Dublin, as the Irish Sea is a good for plaice and cod. We did all right, but the Irish fishermen, especially their fisher foxes, didn't like Italians and Albanians in their waters. However, Wilfred and Winston both fell in love in Ireland and found employment on a local fishing trawler. They both looked so joyful when we left,' says Rossi.

Diabolo smiles from ear to ear, knowing that his friends are happy and safe.

Alberto, excited to be going on another escapade, bypasses the reunited friends to follow the smell of cooking from the cabin's kitchen, pulling his equally excited mother by the hand.

Carlotta looks back, as she steps on to Viaqua, at Mario giving his final orders. Leonardo and Francesco, two of the heroes from the battle of Sant'Agata de' Goti, both wave at Carlotta, who waves back with a big loving smile. Then Carlotta looks up at the bright stars in the sky, and thinks to herself, 'I am now surrounded by friendship and love, not resentment and hatred. That is so beautiful.'

Her positive mindset is broken when she hears a familiar and friendly voice. 'Carlotta, please call my papa. They are just about to serve linguine con cozze di Nonno (linguine and mussels)—one of his favourite dishes,' says the ever-hungry Alberto. Yet Carlotta doesn't need to shout, as the aroma from the ship's kitchen has Mario running like a cub to the fishing trawler.

Mario smiles as he runs past Carlotta and into Viaqua's kitchen. Then the Don Fox screams out in a combination of shock and joy, before bellowing out, 'I thought you had drowned at sea. Everyone thought I had killed you.'

Carlotta walks quickly into the ship's kitchen to see what has happened now. She sees a rather shaken Mario; in front of him is an old white-haired and well-built man with olive skin, in a vest, dirty white apron, crumpled chef hat, donning a pair of jeans that could do with a good wash, a large metal pot of linguine dangling in his right hand, his mouth wide open in total and utter disbelief.

Then he composes himself and says: 'Mario Bandito, as you can see, I never drowned. I fell off the boat by accident the day we went fishing. Being a strong swimmer, I thought I could swim back to the shore and surprise you later. Yet the tide was strong and took me away from Naples and into the Tyrrhenian Sea. I thought I would die, as I believed it was a sign from above cos of all the bad things I have done in my life.

'But then, out of nowhere, a ferry appeared and rescued me. I didn't tell the crew who I was, just in case there was a policeman or two onboard. I just told them I was from Sardinia and I had fallen overboard, so they dropped me off in Cagliari. But after my near-death experience, I was in no rush to go back to my former life. In fact, it was the first time since the age of 15 I felt free, so I stayed on the island. I rented a small room in a cosy house, earning a living as a chef in a small restaurant, Osmosis, in the port.

'Then one day in the restaurant, Rocco and Rossi were having their lunch after docking their ship. We got talking, but the boss sacked me on the spot for chatting. So, Rocco offered me a job as Viaqua's chef, as they were planning a long fishing trip around the Mediterranean. It was only going to be for a few months, but we became like brothers, so I told them about my old life, which didn't disturb them.

'So, after getting that off my chest, I then realised that life on the sea is better than life on the streets of Naples. So, my old friend Mario, Don Vittorio Mosele is dead, Vitto the chef is alive and well.'

Mario smiles then asks with much annoyance, 'Why didn't you get in touch to tell me, your family, your friends that you were alive and well? Why didn't you? Everyone thought that your blood was on my hands.'

Then Mario screams out in anger as he pulls out his trusted pistol from his dark blue tailor-made mohair trousers: 'I should kill you now for the pain, the guilt, I have suffered for years. And all the time, you were cooking and sailing around Europe.'

'No, Mario don't be an idiot,' snaps Carlotta at Mario, knowing full well he has no intention of shooting his one-time friend and former boss.

Mario, seeing his own stupidity passes his pistol to Carlotta, sits down at the dinner table in the ship's kitchen, and starts to weep. Don Vittorio Mosele, now Vitto the chef, walks slowly over to the Don fox, and says with sincerity, 'Mario, I am sorry, I really am, please forgive me.'

Mario looks up at Vitto, smiles a sad smile, then looks down to the ship's wooden floor. Carlotta nudges Vitto gently in the back. The chef quickly glances at the good witch, who nods in the direction of the sad fox, as she mouths the words, 'Carry on.' So he does.

'It is good to see you; you look well and prosperous. This is the first time since I fell overboard that I have returned to Naples. We docked here on Christmas Eve, three days' leave, as no one is buying fish during Christmas. But tomorrow, at the crack of dawn, we set sail for the Bay of Biscay.

'Mario, it was strange seeing the old haunts, but no one recognised me. I thought about visiting my family, you, all my old friends, but it didn't feel right. I didn't want to be the ghost of Christmas Past. But please, dear friend, let's eat and let bygones be bygones. I doubt I will be back again—it's not my home any more. But I did love the fireworks on Christmas Eve; we saw them from afar. Were they at Sant'Agata de' Goti?' asks Vitto, hoping to win Mario's friendship back.

'They were not fireworks. Let me explain,' says Carlotta.

■ ■ ■

Terrified and engrossed by Carlotta's anecdote told over dinner and the predicament that Alberto is in, Rocco, Rossi and Vitto are only too willing to help.

'Don Mario, Madame Silvia and Carlotta, Master Alberto and long-lost friend Diabolo, it will be an honour to sail through the Bay of Biscay and land in England,' says Captain Rocco.

'That is very kind of you. We will pay you double, in dollars, lira or pound notes. I have all three currencies and plenty of them in my bag,' says Mario, now happier and calmer after a generous helping of linguine con cozze di Nonno and a few bottles of Italian beer.

'Just cover our costs,' says Rossi, who is also the ship's bookkeeper.

Mario nods and smiles, especially at Vitto.

'But we must sail now. We can't wait,' says Carlotta in an authoritative manner.

'Full steam ahead,' commands Rocco.

To which Alberto jumps up—but not for joy, but to help himself to more food.

11

Foxham, Here We Come

'Yak,' shrieks Silvia, yet no one is paying attention, because for the past seven and a half days at sea, her husband Mario, her son Alberto, family friend and bodyguard Diabolo, the good witch Carlotta, the ship's captain Rocco, the ship's mate Rossi and the ship's cook, former crime boss Vittorio Mosele (now known as 'Vitto the chef'), have grown accustomed to her whining.

From the ship being too small to the sea swaying too much, Silvia Bandito always found something to complain about. At first, everyone would try to comfort her, but now they don't even bother. Yet with the beautiful white cliffs of Dover coming into view, all on board Viaqua hope that Silvia's continuous moaning will be over. But Mario knows that Silvia will find something new to whinge about when they set off from Dover to Foxham.

Everyone—well, apart from Silvia—has enjoyed the trip from Santa Lucia, Naples, to the white cliffs of Dover. Rocco made just one stop—that was the port of Marseille. Rocco thought it would be better for Viaqua to do their fishing and trading after the trawler had dropped off their passengers in England.

At Marseille, the crew and passengers stocked up on food and drink, and bought Italian newspapers, books, a deck of cards and board games—all paid for by Mario, who also treated everyone to a pizza in the port before they set off.

Diabolo became the undisputed chess master, whilst Rossi excelled as a detective in Cluedo. No one could beat Alberto at dominos, and it was a close first between Rocco and Vitto in draughts. Silvia owned all of London in Monopoly, which cheered her up to a degree, and Mario won a few English pounds with gin rummy.

Carlotta would read classic adventure stories such as *Robinson Crusoe* and *Gulliver's*

Travels during the day. Luckily for the rest of the crew, Carlotta could read French, as the books were purchased in Marseille. In the evening, Carlotta would re-enact these great tales after they had eaten a hearty fish supper, cooked by Vitto, with a lot of help from Mario. Carlotta's performances became the evening's entertainment, for she never failed to amuse and delight all on board. Silvia took charge of cleaning Viaqua, but Diabolo did most, if not all of the work. Rocco steered the ship, with Rossi navigating, whereas Alberto learnt how to use the ship's radio. The crew got so engrossed with the games and their duties that they forgot to see in the New Year, 1958.

With Alberto's newly acquired radio ham skills, Mario asked his son to contact the port office at the bay of Santa Lucia, which Alberto did with great success. From this connection, Mario was able to instruct his gang, from where he received the good news that there hadn't been a reprise attack on Naples. The Witches of Benevento along with the red-cap goblins were nowhere to be seen. All the 'families of Naples,' Mario's crew, the boxing wolf brothers from Benevento Leonardo and Francesco, and the bears of Campania patrolled the region, giving the locals peace of mind. Yet Carlotta warned Mario the witches would be scheming.

Even though thankfully Viaqua had not been attacked while at sea, they were followed sometimes by a flock of black crows, who were flying too close to the ship for Carlotta's liking. So, Carlotta, through the power of magic, asked the seagulls flying above the trawler to see off the black crows; the seagulls were happy to oblige.

Carlotta was right to be wary of the crows, as the Witches of Benevento had summoned the birds—when Carlotta was telling Mario of their need to flee to Foxham in the living room of his apartment in Viale Anton Dohrn on Boxing Day evening, Ettore the black cat, after regaining consciousness from being knocked out by Alberto, was listening in, unnoticed as he lay on the windowsill.

■ ■ ■

'Happy New Year and good morning, Trudi. I thoroughly enjoyed the turkey sandwiches for lunch, and the turkey slices with bubble and squeak for dinner we have had for the last week,' says a happy Chester to Trudi, as he is about to embark on his morning duties as the caretaker of Foxham Care Home for Foxes. It is a job that he relishes, and his nice and happy manner have made him extremely popular with the residents.

Chester's pleasant nature is not just limited to the care home and Foxham, for this fox paid back all the money to his friends from Ipswich that was sent to him when they believed Chester was unable to walk. Moreover, the farmhands from Ipswich often visit Chester in Foxham and Chester visits them in Ipswich, friends forever.

Trudi just smiles and nods, as she prepares to have a New Year's Day stroll across Foxham Common with her grandmother Anna. But Trudi is feeling preoccupied, because during Christmas Eve in Foxham, while the Battle of Sant'Agata de' Goti was taking place, there was a sudden downpour of rain, followed by thunder and lightning. Yet once the battle had finished in Italy, the rain stopped, the clouds parted and the moon started to shine brightly in Foxham. The villagers of Foxham thought it was the weather just being the weather, yet Trudi felt a strange sensation, foretelling that something or someone was coming.

'Trudi, there is something that you need to know,' says Anna, as they both stroll across the common. Anna knows the storm that hit Foxham on Christmas Eve was a sign of Trudi's destiny. But Anna thought she would get Christmas out of the way before telling her granddaughter that she is a good witch who has been given the responsibility of saving the world.

Trudi just nods as her grandmother speaks, believing it is going to be their usual discussion about menus or such like. Then Trudi becomes alert, when she sees Charlie and Owen riding around the common on their new bikes.

Young Charlie and Owen had been banned from owning a bike after the whole village found out that the duo had stolen Chester's bright red bike on the day their trial collapsed at Foxham Magistrates Court. Chester was very hurt, as it was his bravery, testimony and photographs that gave these young foxes their freedom back, which led to the arrest and charge of Penelope Painshill, PC Rex, Mrs Duke and Blades the butcher. Moreover, it took Charlie and Owen many months of grovelling and volunteer work to be finally accepted again by Foxham and their relatives, after the two friends had endured many months of being ostracised.

But Trudi, to this day, still doesn't trust them, especially Charlie. Furthermore, she is annoyed to see them parading about on their new bikes after their parents agreed to lift the ban as if nothing had happened.

'Trudi, are you listening? There is something you need to know,' Anna says in an irate manner.

'What is it, grandmother?' snaps Trudi, glaring at Charlie and Owen as they ride past.

Anna waits until the terrible two are out of earshot. She coughs and clears her throat then says, 'Trudi Milanese, you are a witch.'

'What a horrible thing to say. Wasn't it I who cooked a lovely Christmas dinner? Wasn't it I who, only last night, made you a nice cup of cocoa before bedtime?' says an annoyed and slightly hurt Trudi.

'But you are. Please listen…'

But Trudi stops Anna from finishing her sentence. 'So, you think I fly across the night sky on a broomstick with a black cat, cackling, in a black pointed hat. Thank you, it is nice to know how you truly see your granddaughter. Well, you remind me of the troll that lives underneath the bridge from the Three Billy-Goats Gruff fairy tale,' yells Trudi, which makes Charlie and Owen brake suddenly to witness the commotion going on between grandmother and granddaughter.

'Oh, I do, do I? What a truly wicked and cruel thing to say to the one person, other than your dear departed grandfather, who has shown you nothing but love. Trudi, you're not a bad witch, but a good witch, blessed to do beautiful things in the world, and very soon, you will need these powers,' says Anna annoyed and very hurt by Trudi's comments.

Trudi, who knows deep down that her grandmother is telling her the truth but just doesn't want to believe it, is saddened by her remarks to her grandmother. So, Trudi walks over to hug Anna, which Anna welcomes with open arms. As grandmother and granddaughter cuddle, they both start to cry, which makes Charlie and Owen giggle.

■ ■ ■

'Well, it's good to be on dry land again. And I have had enough fish dinners to last me a lifetime,' declares Silvia as she, Mario, Alberto, Diabolo and Carlotta enter a private carriage from a passageway on a train bound to St Pancras, London, from Dover Priory train station. Mario, who wants an event-free train journey, agrees with her, as do the others.

As the train pulls off, all five of them start to feel sad, as they recall their recent tearful farewell with Rossi, Rocco, and Vitto the chef, at the port of Dover. Then Diabolo tries to raise their spirits by giving everyone a tuna or cheese sandwich and an iced bun that he had bought from a baker's near the train station.

'Once we get to St Pancras, we will have to get something called the under-ground to Liverpool Street. Then a train to Norwich. There isn't a train station in Foxham, so we will have to catch a bus, there is one an hour,' says Carlotta, who asked a stationmaster at Dover Priory how to get to Foxham. The stationmaster was only too keen to help this beautiful Italian Marilyn Monroe lookalike, as he looked up the journey in a directory in the station's office. He had no trouble understanding Carlotta, as she, like Mario, Silvia, and even Alberto, speak good English; it's just Diabolo who struggles with the language.

'We are not getting this thing called the underground nor are we catching a bus. We will hail a taxi, two if we have to,' remarks Silvia.

'Yes, dear,' says Mario, staring at Carlotta and the others with a look of 'anything for a quiet life', as the train gathers speed.

'Game of chess?' enquires Diabolo, eager to show that he is still the chess master.

'Give him a game, Alberto. I am sure his winning streak is bound to come to an end. I will go and get some cold and hot drinks to go with the sandwiches and buns. Compared to the sea journey, we should be in London in the blink of an eye,' says Carlotta in a joyous manner, as she slides the compartment door open, stepping into the train corridor to locate the buffet carriage.

As Carlotta heads to her left, thinking that the buffet carriage might be in that direction, she notices a sinister cloaked figure dressed all in black with round glasses, standing by the toilet in the train's corridor.

'A day prowler, not a spy for Diana,' Carlotta mutters to herself.

Carlotta, like many witches, knows of men and women who call themselves, 'day prowlers'—individuals who have succumbed to the dark side of life and sometimes like to dress up like a character from a horror film, book or comic, which makes it easier for someone in the know, like Carlotta, to spot them. However, spies for the dark side are much harder to spot.

Day prowlers have no special powers, other than the will to inflict evil on everyday folk in any way they see fit. However, more often or not, they are not that mentally or physically strong, so these entities can be easy to overcome. Furthermore, day prowlers are usually pseudo-intellectuals.

■ ■ ■

'One of our infiltrators, Mr Potts, a stationmaster at Dover, has just sent a telegram saying that the traitor Carlotta and the fat fox have boarded a train heading to London,' Diana tells Andriana, Benedetta, Caterina and Ettore the black cat.

So, the stationmaster Mr Potts didn't give Carlotta directions out of the kindness of his heart. No, it is because Mr Potts is a spy. I did say that their spies are hard to spot.

'In the telegram, Mr Potts also says there was a day prowler at the station, ready to follow Carlotta and her silly friends. A brute by the name of Henry Robins is now aboard the same train as the traitor and the fat fox,' adds Diana.

'Shall we get the broomsticks and greet that xxxxx Carlotta when she gets to London then kidnap old fatty?' enquires Andriana.

'What? For you to get knocked out again? That wolf certainly showed you up!' jokes Benedetta.

But Andriana is in no mood for gags. Thus, she leaps over the kitchen table at a villa near their original home of Castello e Torre di Montesarchio and tries to strangle Benedetta, who fights back hard. Caterina, who is feeling now that she should be the head of the coven, due to Diana's recent disaster in letting Alberto escape, attempts to pull Andriana off Benedetta, but with no success, while Ettore meows, 'Stop! Stop!'

Diana looks at the two red-capped goblins, who are also in the kitchen, awaiting their orders from the coven's leader. Diana points at the fight and shouts out, 'Stop it.' So the red-capped goblins proceed to break up the fight.

Yet the red-capped goblins are unaware that Andriana is a seasoned boxer. So, when one of them is sucker-punched by the witch, which puts him on the floor, this usually vicious red-capped goblin is in shock. Therefore, Diana is left with no choice but to get physically involved. This is something she doesn't like to do, as she prefers others to do her dirty work. Diana pulls Andriana back by her long raven hair, who screams an unearthly high-pitched screech—so much so, a few bottles of wine on the shelves shatter. Meanwhile, Benedetta, shocked by the recent fight, is held back by the red-capped goblin (the one that didn't get knocked down).

'Enough,' orders Diana, annoyed with the bout. 'Look, we have much work to do. We are going to plunge the world into eternal darkness.'

Diana's remarks are met by a meow of 'Hear, hear!' from Ettore. The poor black cat receives a clip around the ear from Diana for his enthusiasm, which makes Ettore whimper.

'Before I was rudely interrupted, I was going to say we will make this world a dark one, full of witches, warlocks and ghoulies,' declares Diana.

'Yes, but you cannot be leader, for it is I, Caterina, daughter of Monica, the original head of the Witches of Benevento, who is truly blessed to take this world into darkness,' proclaims Caterina.

Ettore the cat doesn't say anything; he just moves closer to his original mistress, hoping that Caterina will take over. Ettore, since he was a kitten with the original Witches of Benevento, has often switched alliances.

'Yes, your bloodline is great, but you lack the vision and the strength to fulfil the true prophecy of darkness,' states Diana.

'Well, you've hardly done a great job. You let that ugly fat fox escape from here with the traitor on one of those horrible scooters—a hairdryer on wheels. My mother would have not allowed that to happen,' snaps Caterina.

'Your mother was burnt alive at the stake. That execution made us witches go into hiding, where we became the stuff of legends and silly folklore. So, don't start preaching to me about your birthright,' retorts Diana.

'My mother died for the cause,' cries out Caterina.

'If your mother hadn't got drunk and opened her mouth at a local inn, we wouldn't be chasing some stupid fox across Europe. Your mother brought nothing but shame to all witches,' snaps Diana.

Caterina, unable to contain her anger, runs over to Diana and they both start to fight, much to the amusement of the red-capped goblins, Andriana, Benedetta and Ettore. Then the deep, booming, self-assured voice of a man pronounces from the kitchen's door, 'Stop this child's play.'

All four witches, the two red-capped goblins and the one black cat stop, turn and see standing in the doorway a tall, strong-looking and handsome man with a pointed nose, slicked-back grey hair and a well-trimmed grey beard, dressed in a purple suit with a frilly white shirt underneath and the shiniest black pointed shoes that you will ever see.

'I am Enoch, the messenger of "you know who", and soon I will be the ruler of the Earth. Now kneel,' orders the well-dressed man.

Diana glances at the rest of the coven, the cat and the two goblins with fear, as she leads them by kneeling first.

'Excellent. You two red-capped goblins will now be called Edor and Eder. You will be my bodyguards. Now, come and stand beside me.' The red-capped goblins, Edor and Eder, stand up and eagerly take their places. 'Ettore, you are now my cat. Come and be stroked by your new master,' orders Enoch. Ettore leaps up from kneeling and into the open arms of Enoch, who slowly strokes the cat. Ettore pokes his tongue out at his former mistresses.

Enoch then gazes at the witches, who are still kneeling, with a look of frustration and says, 'Diana, Andriana, Benedetta and Caterina, you had the chosen fox in your grasp, a traitor in your midst, yet they escaped. You called upon a brave army of red-capped goblins, but you were defeated by a gang of common criminals, a disloyal witch, a legion of well-dressed bears, simple villagers and two boxing wolves. I know that the turncoat, the fox and his family are now in that horrible country England, heading to Foxham, full of nasty foxes. I should have Edor and Eder hack you into little pieces with their battleaxes for your failure, but I will let you live. Therefore, you have been granted one last chance to fulfil the prophecy.'

The witches in unison breathe a huge sigh of relief.

'I am not sparing you out of pity. Trust me, I wanted to punish you with your lives, but the powers below stopped me,' says an authoritative Enoch as he points to the floor.

Then he continues: 'As the sight of you makes me very sick, I have arranged for you to fly to England this very evening in the private plane of a wicked and rich friend of mine, from a disused airfield 10 miles or so from here. When you land, you will have a few months to gather an army of all that is evil that walks in England.

'Then, on 6th April, you invade Foxham—and not before, as we know sacrificing Alberto Bandito before then would be a waste. You must kill everyone in the village, from foxes to humans. But spare the fox witch called Trudi Milanese and the traitor, for they must witness all the death and destruction.

'Then at the turret of the old medieval tower on Foxham Common at the given hour, you finally sacrifice Alberto Bandito. Thus, the prophecy will be fulfilled. I will remain here with Ettore, Edor and Eder to spread fear across Naples and beyond. For this to go according to plan, a new leader is needed.'

'It is me,' says an eager yet foolish Caterina.

'Shut up and never speak to me unless I grant you permission. No, not one of you is fit to lead. But your mother was… and is. Please welcome the true queen of witches: Monica.'

A beautiful raven-haired woman with dark brown eyes, in a white blouse, purple skirt and beautiful brown leather hand-woven sandals, enters from the kitchen doorway. Edor and Eder move back, allowing this striking woman to stand next to the dashing yet dastardly man.

'Mamma,' cries out Caterina.

'Silence, child. You have failed the family name. I have risen from the ashes… to fulfil the prophecy of "i sogni dei bambini",' bellows the resurrected Monica.

Monica's dramatic entrance and equally dramatic announcement motivates the witches to get off their knees and cackle like they never have before. The witches' new leader joins in with pleasure with the evil laughter. Edor and Eder start to grunt loudly, as they punch their battleaxes into the air. Ettore meows with all his might in his master's arms. Enoch smiles, standing proudly amongst this rise of evil.

12

The Road to Foxham

Carlotta, fearless as ever, heads on towards the day prowler, Henry Robins. A disciple of all that is wicked, yet useless at the implementation of evil, the tragic Henry Robins is a nondescript accountant at Hart and Sons in Bethnal Green.

Henry Robins arrives at the office spot on time and leaves dead on time. Henry Robins eats the same sandwich fillings on the same day with the same flavoured crisps at the same time every day, 12.30pm, at the same desk. Henry Robins dresses in the same dull grey suit, same dull grey tie, same creased white shirt in the same pair of unpolished brown shoes. Every working day is the same for Henry Robins.

For the short walk from work to his small yet tidy bedsit in Hackney, everyone from the pretty women to the nosey pensioners do not notice Henry Robins—to them, he is invisible. Yet any soul who walks this Earth, be it a human, a fox or suchlike, through determination and love can become a beautiful soul who endears people. Yet Robins, with a severe and unfounded superiority complex, believes it is the world's fault that no one sees him.

Then a few years ago, one evening, Henry Robins watched a rerun of a film, *Mark of the Vampire*, starring Bela Lugosi, at a small cinema in Soho. Thus, Henry Robins in the evenings and at weekends—well, apart from Sunday mornings, as he must visit his mother in Harrow—drops the look of the dreary accountant and adopts that of a vampire, just like his screen idol, Bela Lugosi.

Thankfully, Henry Robins is yet to do anything sinful so, as he waits to hatch a dastardly plan, he passes the time by walking around the haunted and sinister areas of London. Henry Robins' favourite stroll is around Whitechapel as he retraces the steps of Jack the Ripper. And this is how Henry Robins met Gilberto the crow,

leader of the Neapolitan crows, who was ordered by Diana to follow Carlotta and her friends aboard Viaqua as they sailed from Naples to England, and when he got to England, Gilberto was instructed to find a day prowler.

■ ■ ■

Unfortunately for Gilberto, he landed in the garden of the villa near the Castello e Torre di Montesarchio on Boxing Day evening, looking for some tasty Christmas leftovers. At the same time in the garden, Ettore, back from Naples, was telling

Diana of Carlotta's plan. Diana, upon seeing the black crow, knew he could be of some use as a spy and a messenger in exchange for two whole margherita pizzas. Gilberto's passion for pizza is notorious around Naples.

Diana cast a spell of telepathy on the crow, so she is able to communicate with him, and she cast a second spell that gives Gilberto the ability to speak fluent Italian and English, just like a human, for when he finds a day prowler. The second spell made Gilberto grow six inches taller. Why? Not even Diana knows.

■ ■ ■

After avoiding the seagulls and seeing that Viaqua was a day or so away from Dover, Gilberto broke away from his gang of crows, and flew towards the white cliffs in less than half a day. The crows of Dover told the Italian crow to go to London, as no evil prowled in Dover.

Consequently, Gilberto found Henry Robins by accident on Friday evening, around Gunthorpe Street, which used to be called George Yard until October 1912—a place in London where Jack the Ripper did away with Martha Turner, also known as Martha Tabram, on 7th August 1888.

When Gilberto saw Henry Robins in Gunthorpe Street, acting like the bogey man, waiting to pounce on a passer-by, Gilberto thought he had found an evil day prowler. But luckily for the world, Gilberto's judgment was all wrong. Yet Henry Robins sure looked the part.

When Gilberto asked Henry Robins if he was a day prowler, ready to fight a witch and kidnap a fox, Henry Robins fainted as he, like most humans, had never heard a crow speak before, especially one with an Italian accent.

Gilberto pecked Henry Robins' forehead with his rather fat beak and soon, Robins gained consciousness. Then the awakened Henry Robins boasted falsehoods of wicked accomplishments and nasty schemes in the planning. Gilberto, who was not that impressed, told Robins to leave London immediately and head to Dover, as Viaqua would be docking there within the day. The useless day prowler wasted no time in obeying the crow, for he hated the foxes that lived around East London, and to kidnap one would satisfy his prejudice.

That very evening, Gilberto befriended some kind East London crows above a pub near Whitechapel called The Blind Beggar. These feathered creatures kindly allowed Gilberto to stay in their nests in the pub's gutter, Gilberto was truly thankful. But in the morning, Gilberto awoke with a feeling of guilt and shame.

■ ■ ■

'The fox will die,' mutters Henry Robins to Carlotta in the train corridor, believing this is his finest hour. Yet Robins has forgotten that his orders are just to follow Carlotta and her friends, and not to kill Alberto. Moreover, Henry Robins stops himself from fully attacking Carlotta, as he is overwhelmed by her uncanny resemblance to Marilyn Monroe.

Carlotta, who only a few years ago was living a carefree and fun life but now has the huge responsibility of saving the world, replies with confidence and with a pseudo-American accent: 'To kill him, you have to kill me first… chum.'

'With pleasure,' declares Henry Robins, as he pulls out a silver knife that gleams brightly on this sunny day in January. Carlotta steps back, giving herself enough room to use her legs so that she can kick and disarm her attacker.

Henry Robins, for the first time ever, feels power.

Robins hunches down slightly, with both shoulders rising to his ear lobes. He tilts his head to his right, as he lunges forward with the knife. Carlotta ducks the knife attack but is not able to kick Robins due to the train's narrow corridor.

Henry Robins' adrenaline is pulsing to the rattling of the train and the wind blasting through the slidden-down carriage window. Robins smiles as he thrusts the silver knife towards Carlotta. But thanks to her amazing dancing skills, Carlotta is too fast for him… until she slips on a wet patch, probably spilled tea, and falls on her backside.

Now powerless and helpless, Carlotta believes it is only a matter of seconds before she is hurt or even worse. Suddenly, she hears flapping wings, and a rather overweight and larger-than-usual crow flies through the train's window, and with his beak, takes the knife out of Robins' hand.

Henry Robins screams like a child who has had their toy taken away, for he has lost the power to a crow that, a day ago, Robins thought had given him a purpose in life. Gilberto, with his beak, throws the knife out of the train and starts to peck Robins hard on the forehead, flapping his wings in Robins' face. As he does, this man and crow both start to spin around in the narrow corridor.

Carlotta quickly jumps up, opens the train door, puts both her hands firmly on

Robins' shoulders, spins around on her heels like she is dancing to a rock 'n' roll record. Now, Henry Robins, with Gilberto still pecking his forehead, is facing out of the train and towards the speeding scenery.

Gilberto, sensing what is going on, flies over Robins' head and back into the train. Carlotta, with all her might, pushes the failed day prowler, who shrieks as he soars out of the train. The loud scream makes Mario, Silvia, Diabolo and Alberto come out of their carriage to see what the commotion is all about.

'He didn't have a ticket,' jokes Carlotta, as she slams the train door shut. Everyone laughs, including Gilberto, who is now sitting on Carlotta's right shoulder, giving her some discomfort due to his size and weight. Nevertheless, a firm friendship has been formed in a moment of panic and madness.

Alberto, as jolly as ever, looks at the crow, and says, 'Hi, I'm Alberto. I know you. You're that crow that loves pizza. I've seen you flying above the pizzerias in Naples.'

Gilberto straight away recognises Alberto. This makes him feel guilty, as two nights ago, he was on the side of their enemy. But after spending a night in the gutter of The Blind Beggar, Gilberto grew a conscience, therefore he changed sides.

The crow smiles at the friendly fox and says, 'Yes, my name is Gilberto, and I have been given the spell of speech. Do you have a slice of pizza, please, Alberto?'

'No, England doesn't seem to have many pizzerias, but maybe one day they will. But we do have some nice tuna and cheese sandwiches and iced buns. Would you like some, Gilberto, our new friend?' asks Alberto, as friendly as ever.

'Yes, please,' replies a delighted Gilberto.

■ ■ ■

After the eventful and triumphant encounter with Henry Robins, Alberto and co are looking forward to a less hectic journey from Liverpool Street Station to Norwich, where they can enjoy the sights and eat their Italian food, as all of them, from Carlotta to Diabolo, are missing the tastes of home.

After getting out of a crammed black taxi, it was Diabolo, with his powerful nose, that found an Italian deli near Liverpool Street Station, owned by brother and sister foxes Piero and Lucia from Palermo. For the group from Naples, it was like Christmas Day, as Silvia bought Italian bread, garlic, olive oil, pasta, gorgonzola, taleggio and tinned Italian tomatoes. Mario bought salami, soppressata and prosciutto, while

Diabolo bought meatballs and olives, Carlotta bought a selection of Italian cakes. Alberto and Gilberto ate a pizza in the deli, as well as having one cooked and put in a large brown and horizontal box for the train journey. All of them believe that Foxham will be just traditional British food. But Trudi and Anna have brought a taste of Italy to Foxham, which will certainly make this lot incredibly happy.

Just before the Naples Six went mad in Piero and Lucia's deli, Silvia found a departmental store, and paid for everyone, apart from Gilberto, to have a change of clothes and a selection of new suitcases. Silvia was not being mean to Gilberto; it's just he doesn't wear clothes. So, Silvia bought him a small white cap, which the departmental store made some adjustments to fit Gilberto's head, which he now wears with delight. Everyone has complimented him on how good he looks in his new cap.

Gilberto was invited straight away to join the entourage by Mario after he had saved Carlotta from Henry Robins. Gilberto was only too happy to accept and was pleased to take a rest from flying.

As their first train journey ended, Gilberto informed Carlotta of how Diana had tricked him into following them and seeking a day prowler, and how worried he was about the two spells cast upon him, as well as saying sorry.

Gilberto was not bothered about being telepathic as Diana was trying to contact him, yet it was through this ability that Gilberto was able to track down Henry Robins. But he did not want to lose the ability to speak. Carlotta wholeheartedly accepted the apology, broke Diana's spells, and cast a new 'ability to speak' spell, adding German, Spanish, Chinese and French to English and Italian.

Gilberto is chuffed to be a multilingual crow and still be six inches taller than the average one.

As Gilberto and his new friends sit in their train carriage, looking forward to their food and picturesque train journey, they hear a confident, powerful yet friendly male voice. 'I take it all of you are going to Foxham?'

They turn to see a black man with a beaming smile, in a khaki three-button suit, light blue shirt and a white pork-pie hat, with nicely polished brown brogues. Standing by his side in the doorway of the train carriage is a pretty and elegant black woman in a halterneck, light-blue, polka-dot dress with a light-blue pillbox hat, white nappa gloves and a pair of shiny brown low-heeled t-strap ballroom shoes.

Next to her is a small and smiling black boy in a short-sleeved white shirt, grey shorts and brown leather sandals.

All six of them smile at the charming and well-dressed strangers, before Mario responds, saying, 'Yes, sir, my family and three good friends are travelling to Foxham…'

'To stay with Charles Reynard, sir?' cuts in the man.

'Yes, to see Charles. Please call me Mario. This is my wife Silvia, my son Alberto, my good friend and right-hand Doberman Diabolo, a close and loyal friend of the family Carlotta, and our new friend Gilberto, the first talking crow. We are all from Naples and nearby. And you, sir, are?' replies Mario, in perfect English.

'Thank you, Mario. I am George, George Campbell. This is my wife Betty and my son Bernard. We are from Notting Hill; Betty and I are originally from Jamaica, but Bernard is a London boy.'

'I would love to go to Jamaica,' squeaks Gilberto.

'Ha, Gilberto, I am sure you will. You look good in that cap. My wife and I came over 10 years ago, docked in Tilbury. I am—well, was—a Tube driver and Betty worked in a ticket office before we had this bundle of joy,' says George, as he points to his son Bernard, who smiles upon hearing this remark.

'Where are our manners? Please take your seats. I know it is a little cramped, but we are three foxes, one dog, one human and a crow, so we will have room. Also, we have some nice Italian food,' says Silvia. However, her closing sentence makes Alberto and Gilberto nervous—as nice as the Campbells seem, Alberto and Gilberto do not want to share their pizza. Yet their fear is confirmed, when Silvia adds, 'Alberto, Gilberto, make sure to give a slice of pizza to our new friends.'

'That is exceedingly kind of you, Alberto and Gilberto,' says Betty, as she takes her seat.

Alberto and Gilberto nervously smile at everyone, as they reluctantly open their pizza box to share their mushroom pizza.

■ ■ ■

'So, you are going to be living and working in Foxham?' asks Mario.

'Yes, Mario. I am overseeing the building of the train station for Foxham. A few years ago, we went to Foxham for a holiday. Being of this skin colour, some places in England do not welcome us. Yet one friend had been to Foxham, and said the foxes were so kind—cheeky and naughty, but kind'

'That is foxes for you!' says Alberto, who makes everyone chuckle in the carriage, apart from Gilberto and Diabolo, who have gone to buy some cold and hot drinks for everyone. Carlotta could sense there were no day prowlers or spies on the train, so she knew they would be safe; she also knows they are both good fighters.

'So, we went, had a great holiday, no signs warning us off,' says Betty with a sense of fear.

'Signs? What do you mean by signs?' asks a concerned Silvia.

'"No Blacks, No Dogs, No Foxes, No Irish." You see them all over London, in boarding houses, hotels,' answers Betty, as she takes off her hat, to place it neatly on her lap.

'That is wrong,' screams Alberto, outraged by the injustice.

'I agree,' adds Carlotta.

'Yes, it is. That is why my people live in Notting Hill and Brixton—it was the cheapest place given to us to live as no one else wanted to live there. The people are great and I loved my job, but the flats are sometimes rooms with 10 people living in them, and the landlords are so mean on rent day, which is often a Friday night, as we usually get paid Friday afternoon. It is the same for the foxes in Hackney and Bethnal Green, for it is still the only part of London where foxes can live,' says George with profundity.

'I never looked at it like that before. I thought the foxes I know from East London love living there,' says Mario.

'They probably do, as places like Notting Hill, Hackney and all that are great, because the people, foxes, dogs make it fun,' says George in a more cheerful mood.

'Just like Naples, it's the people who give it its beauty and magic,' says Carlotta in a proud manner.

'True. Just like Foxham,' says Betty.

'Talking about Foxham, how come you got a job there with Charles Reynard?' enquires Silvia in a friendly tone.

'Good question, Silvia. Luck and courage, I guess. Well, when I started working as a Tube driver, I would go to an evening class in Hammersmith, not far from Notting Hill, to study engineering. I wanted to be an engineer in Jamaica. Without being big-headed, I got my diploma but it's hard for a black man to get a good engineering job in London.

'Anyway, we are in The Six Bells, eating some lovely roast chicken for lunch. Then

Charles comes in, dead pleased as he buys a drink for everyone, then he announces that Norwich Council are building some new rail lines and train stations, and Foxham will get a single-track train station five miles from the village centre. Everyone cheers, which makes me think I have a good opportunity here.

'So, I walk over to Charles, shake his paw, tell him about my diploma, and that I would like a job with the building of the new train station. Charles then invites me, Betty and Bernard that evening to Fox Hill Hall for dinner and a conversation. His wife Kaye and son Foxy kept my family company whilst Charles and I spoke in his study. At the end of the meeting, I was offered a well-paid job as the head of engineering, Betty part-time work in the office, with a lovely cottage looking out onto Foxham Common. I am so happy,' says a delighted George.

'That is wonderful for you and your family,' says Mario sincerely, as the crime boss is starting to learn that kindness is a beautiful thing.

'We know Charles and Kaye well—they stayed with us in Naples just before Alberto was born and once we stayed with them at Fox Hill Hall. Alberto was too young to travel with us, so Diabolo, who has adored Alberto from the day he was born, looked after him—they are like brothers. I like Charles and Kaye, his son Foxy and his family, but as for Ferdy, no,' remarks Silvia.

'Ha, everyone is wary of Ferdy, a real rascal, and his son Charlie causes a lot of problems in Foxham—a very rude and bad fox,' reveals Betty.

'Charlie was just a small, cute cub when we were last there. It is so sad to hear how he has turned out,' sighs Silvia.

'Charlie is just a young foolish fox; I am sure he will grow out of it. So, this is yours and Mario's second trip to Foxham and you decided to take your son and friends for a holiday there?' asks George.

'Kind of,' says Carlotta, knowing what lays ahead…

13

Foxham, We Have Arrived

The Witches of Benevento were scheduled to fly out of Naples to England on a Piper PA-22 from a disused airfield. The small aircraft is owned by a wicked and wealthy man, Sir Henry Hazleton, a devoted worshipper of Enoch, currently residing at his villa outside Naples. However, much to the witches' dismay, the flight was cancelled because, when the five witches arrived at the airfield, Stefano Romano, a seasoned pilot who had no idea that they were witches, refused to fly them as the plane is a four-seater. Stefano knew that extra passengers, along with extra baggage, would endanger himself and the passengers.

Stefano Romano, a handsome and well-built man with dark skin and neatly cut dark hair who recently turned 40, had been a pilot for Regia Aeronautica during the war. Stefano did not enjoy the intense and bloody conflict, but now, in peacetime, he is a happy man, as after the war, he married the girl of his dreams, Aria. From this blissful wedlock, Aria gave birth to two daughters—Gabriella and Beatrice—and Stefano loves all of them more than anything in the world.

Stefano was stimulated by the thrill of flying between the Earth and the sun, after reading several comics as a young teenager. That is why in 1937, he enlisted with Regia Aeronautica, but Stefano did not envisage that the world would become a dark place two years later.

So, with the desire to fly but not to fight, after the war Stefano sought work as a pilot with a private airline that boasts many wealthy clients in Europe, from Sir Henry Hazleton to Mario Bandito. Stefano quickly gained a reputation as an excellent and reliable pilot, which has resulted in him being in gainful employment.

And now Stefano is considering setting up on his own, with Mario being a possible investor. Mario is known to fund businesses and entrepreneurs in Naples, like Charles Reynard in Foxham. But one thing Stefano will not do in his flying career is to bend the rules. Okay, Stefano might bend them with his tax returns, just like Ferdy in Foxham. Moreover, despite the number of bribes Stefano has been offered over the years, he plays it by the book when it comes to flying.

So, when the witches screamed at Stefano with insults and threats when he refused to fly them, their words of hatred did not faze him in the slightest. Stefano just laughed, which frustrated the witches further. Thus, Stefano turned his back on the Witches of Benevento and walked towards his silver Lancia Aurelia B20, a dashing car for a dashing man.

· · ·

'Kill him,' Monica orders Caterina.

'Yes, mamma,' says the obedient daughter, believing that slaughtering this innocent pilot will get her into her mother's good books.

Caterina slowly creeps up with a small knife in her right hand to the unsuspecting Stefano, who is now thinking about spending a lovely dinner with his family, as opposed to flying over the English Channel with five mad women. But Caterina is startled, as the bright headlamps of two Vespas and the headlamp of an Iso Isettacarro pickup truck shine in hers and Stefano's direction, who puts his right hand over his eyes to block out the light. Yet Caterina can make out the silhouettes of two wolves on scooters and two bears in the pickup truck cabin, and a few more in the open cargo box at the back.

'Oh no, it is those pesky wolves and bears. Run!' Caterina screams. Stefano, upon hearing her shriek, turns around to see the witches fleeing, making him laugh as they do. Then Stefano turns back towards his car, and as he does, a wolf on a Vespa slowly approaches him.

■ ■ ■

'So, you are the five that are meant to plunge this Earth into darkness. Ha! You should have slit the pilot's throat and flown the plane yourselves. Edor and Eder have their axes ready to take your heads off,' shouts Enoch so loudly on the telephone in the kitchen that his red-capped goblin bodyguards and Ettore the cat run out of the dark wood drawing room, with new velvet curtains and carpet, where they were enjoying an evening of drinking brandy and talking all things horrible, and into the hallway.

Monica, trembling and frustrated that her return to Earth has not been as successful as she had predicted, meekly replies, 'Oh, master, we are terribly sorry. We will go to Naples International Airport and catch the next available flight to London. Please spare us, for the wolves and bears took us by surprise.'

Enoch pauses, knowing that if he reports another failure to his master, he may also be perceived as a liability and punished accordingly. So, Enoch in his most stern voice, as he does not want Monica to sense his fear, replies, 'I grant you permission, but one more failure and I will personally punish you.'

Monica moves her mouth away from the telephone to let out a huge sigh of relief, then moves her mouth back to the telephone and says, 'Thank you, master. Master, maybe to save time and money, we could fly to England on our broomsticks?'

Enoch, now overwhelmed and drained from the whole scenario, calmly says, 'No,' and puts the receiver down. Enoch shouts out, 'Ettore, get in here! You and I are going on a trip,' as it has dawned on Enoch that a surprise visit from him and the black cat to England would make sure that the job of taking over the world is done with the proper care and attention needed.

Ettore, who now walks upright and has grown a foot in length, due to a growth and 'perfect speech' spell cast by Enoch, strolls into the kitchen, donning his new, wide-brimmed cavalier hat that the cat found in the villa's cellar that was made for a child, not warfare.

■ ■ ■

Enoch and Ettore sit crammed on the back seat of a white Fiat 600 with Pippo Stacchini, a taxi driver with a car that is an accident waiting to happen.

When Enoch announced to Ettore that they were going to England and they would be flying from Naples International Airport, not a private plane, it was the cat's responsibility to arrange the transport.

The reason for a commercial flight was due to the fact that Enoch was truly annoyed with Sir Henry Hazleton. Enoch believed that Sir Henry had failed terribly in choosing a pilot who was not drawn to the dark side. So, he sent Edor and Eder not to kill Sir Hazleton but to teach him a harsh lesson, and to send a message to anyone who might fail Enoch in the future.

Ettore telephoned his friends at l'Diuto Del Diavolo, a group of ghouls who disguised themselves as humans and for the right price can make people suffer or disappear. But this business has been slow for a year or so, as the demand for revenge isn't as popular or as lucrative as it once was. So, these ghouls now run a taxi service from Naples and her provinces to the airport.

When Ettore told Enoch the cost for their airport service, Enoch screamed, 'Go out to a bar and find me a man who will drive us to the airport for the price of a bottle of beer and a slice of pizza, not a bottle of champagne and a plate of oysters.' Ettore, shocked and annoyed by Enoch, went out on his bright yellow bike that he bought the other day after growing a foot taller, thanks to the power of magic.

Ettore is looking forward to the trip to England. As well as doing some skulduggery, Ettore can't wait to go sightseeing, eat fish and chips and roast beef with Yorkshire pudding, and order his former mistresses around, as Enoch has made him second in command. Also, Ettore is looking forward to knocking Alberto out with one punch—for in his mind, the fox took him by surprise and when he was a tad drunk.

So, on his bike and wearing his musketeer hat, Ettore cycles with haste past Sant'Agata de' Goti, as not only does he remember the recent battle here, Ettore also remembers seeing Monica being burnt at the stake, two centuries ago in this village. Ettore will fear this place until the world is under the curse from the Witches of Benevento, Enoch and Enoch's master.

Within 15 minutes, Ettore is in the nearby village of Capellino. As he pulls into the village, he sees a darkly lit bar and through the nicotine-stained window, the cat observes a few men with their heads down as they drink their beer in silence. Ettore, confident with his newfound leadership and hat, gets off his bike, props it on the wall outside the bar, and walks in. 'I am looking for a man to drive Signor Enoch and me to the airport. For this job, you will be handsomely rewarded in beer, pizza and money,' says Ettore in a high-pitched voice, like he is reciting a sentence from a classic adventure novel.

There are a few mutters, until Pippo Stacchini, who has just dropped off a customer from Naples in Capellino, replies in the same manner of Ettore. 'I accept your offer, for I will drive you and Signor Enoch to the airport for two bottles of beer, three slices of pizza and 1,000 lira.'

Ettore replies, 'My good man: one bottle of beer, a large slice of pizza and 500 lira. You will also be able to say that "It was I who drove the great Signor Enoch and the amazing Ettore, the cat in the hat, to the airport," for that is priceless and timeless.'

Pippo, slightly merry and in need of a pizza slice and some money to buy groceries in the morning, answers, 'Sir, I accept your offer. Now take me to Signor Enoch.'

Ettore bows down, taking off his hat with his right paw and waving it over his left shoulder. Then Ettore straightens up, places his hat back on his head, and says, 'Thank you, sir. As time is pressing, we will have to put my yellow bike in your magnificent machine.' With that, Ettore leaves the bar, followed by Pippo. Ettore knows he will have to pay the 500 lira out of his own savings, as Enoch is only prepared to offer beer and pizza, but not money.

∎ ∎ ∎

If Pippo had fixed the brakes as he should have, then the car, along with him and the two passengers with their suitcases in the boot, may not have nosedived into a two-foot sloping ditch on a sharp bend in the road just before Naples International Airport. But he hadn't, due to his daily hangovers and lazy attitude, so the car did crash, making Pippo, an evil underworld lord and a black cat in a cavalier hat scream upon impact.

There was a slight sigh of relief when all three realised that it was a shallow, grassed ditch with soft soil, which helped to minimise the accident. Pippo touched the top of his head and felt a slight trickle of blood; Enoch was in shock, but not hurt. Ettore, due to his size, felt no pain, yet when the car hit the ditch, the top of his head went through the top of his cavalier hat, making Ettore cry like a kitten.

Outraged, Enoch climbed out of the car, which was at an angle, and with brute force he opened the slightly bent boot, pulled out his suitcase and Ettore's, then said with anger, 'We will have to walk.' Pippo didn't say a word, as he knew that the bottle of beer, the slice of pizza and the lira were now out of the question.

• • •

Yallery Brown, the mischievous spirit, bored from his wrongdoings in Lancashire as he is unable to scare any farmers or farmhands as they have finally grown wise to his misdoings, feels the sudden urge to catch a train to Norwich, as something is telling him that his services are needed.

■ ■ ■

The taxi journey from Norwich Station to Foxham required two taxis as there were eight people, as both George's family and Mario's entourage needed to get to the scenic and lively village.

The two taxis are now stationary, with the drivers waiting impatiently outside The Six Bells public house, as George and Mario are arguing who will pick up the fare, for Mario wants to be generous and so does George. Then Silvia and Betty, who have become good friends in a short space of time, suggest that they pay for a taxi each. George and Mario both smile and agree, much to the relief of the taxi drivers, who just want to pick up another customer.

Charles has arranged drinks and food for everyone in the village to celebrate the Campbells moving to Foxham. However, due to all the excitement and travelling, Mario has forgotten to call Charles and let him know that he and his small entourage are coming, and they will need accommodation. But Mario knows getting lodgings in Foxham will not be a problem.

'Hurrah for George, Betty and Bernard,' declares Kaye Reynard as all the Campbells walk into The Three Bells. All three smile with delight when the whole village cheers them, including Ferdy—for one evening, Horace the landlord has again temporarily lifted Ferdy's ban. The last time Horace allowed Ferdy into his pub was for the evening Charles Reynard met Winston Churchill many years ago. But from tomorrow lunchtime, Horace will reinstate the ban.

Everyone is looking forward to some great food, thanks to Kaye, Anna and Trudi: a selection of scotch eggs, pork pies, cold meats, sandwiches with an assortment of coleslaw, potato salad, and bubble and squeak; Italian food, mainly lasagne and pizza, as everyone in Foxham loves pizzas; and jerk chicken, with rice and peas, as George, on his last visit to Foxham to discuss his new job with Charles in more detail, introduced Trudi one lunchtime at Milano's to the joys of Jamaican food.

There will be a good selection of beer, rum, pop and such like, served with pleasure by Horace and his staff. The evening's entertainment will come in the form of a skiffle band hailing from Liverpool called The Quarrymen: three lads, John, Paul and George, who are travelling around England looking for bookings. Ferdy is thinking about becoming their manager, but John is not that keen. And everyone will laugh out loud tonight, thanks to a young fox comedian, in a green Victorian frock coat, white shirt and a red cravat, called Basil Brush, who says, 'Boom, boom!' at the end of each joke. Charles believes that Basil Brush and The Quarrymen will be phenomenally successful in the next decade, the 60s.

And, of course, it will not be a joyous occasion without the wonderful folk of Foxham having a ball.

Chester Brown, in his new suit, is here enjoying a pork pie, his favourite, with a nice pint of ale. All the Cambridges are present—Oliver, Victoria and their two sons, Thomas and Owen. The Painshills have also come to the pub, but, of course, without Penelope, the corrupt magistrate, who is remanded in custody, as she awaits trial on the charges of corruption, preventing the cause of justice and a few more.

Charles pointed out to the villagers that her husband Sebastian, her son Henry and daughter Isabella were none the wiser to her ways, so no one bears a grudge. Sebastian, along with his children, had planned on leaving Foxham, but Charles said it was best that they stayed, as he and his family are happy here.

Boris Bates, out of his butler's uniform, is enjoying a plate of cold chicken with bubble and squeak, as is Sergeant Ali, who is off duty, along with his retired father Brutus and his wife Dot. Foxy and his wife Sandy and their two boys, Hector and Arnold, are also here, and Foxy is now the doctor for Foxham with a new surgery.

Reggie, who has apologised no end to Charlie and Owen, is present. Everyone is pleased, as he is always the life and soul of a knees-up at The Six Bells.

Otto, the former magistrates clerk, is here eating a scotch egg with some crisps. After the infamous trial of Charlie and Owen, Otto, thanks to his father in Norway getting him a new passport and finding a copy of the letter with a firm job offer, is now working at last in the accounts department of Norwich City FC. Otto loves his job, as he gets a free seat every time Norwich City plays at home. Norwich City has a strong fox support, due to the big fox community in Norfolk, as does West Ham, because of the many foxes that live and work around East London. So, for any match between Norwich City and West Ham, there are always many foxes in the stadium.

In fact, dear reader, the list is quite long of who's in attendance. Perhaps it would have been easier to write who hasn't shown up—and that is no one, for everyone is here, and despite the cold January evening, some of the villagers are in the marquee in the beer garden, which is nicely heated with a few paraffin heaters. At the back of the marquee is a small stag, and in half an hour, Basil will make the villagers laugh, then an hour later, The Quarrymen will make them dance. For tonight only, The Six Bells will close when it closes.

But before the entertainment starts, most of the inhabitants of Foxham are in the saloon bar, whilst the snug bar is where the food is, with Trudi standing watch. For no one in Foxham will dare argue with her, as Trudi has already removed a pork pie from Chester's plate, for she believed he was being greedy. Trudi looked over Boris's shoulder when he was helping himself to cold bubble and squeak, just to make sure he did not take any liberties.

∎ ∎ ∎

After the hearty cheers for the Campbells, there are loud gasps as Mario and Silvia walk in. Even though they visited Foxham a few years ago and Mario was charming, the folk of Foxham were wary of him. The mood quickly changes to joy when Alberto walks into The Six Bells, as the sight of this jolly and happy fox makes everyone clap and cheer. Then there are more loud gasps when Diabolo menacingly strolls in. He and Sergeant Ali's eyes meet, they both nod at each other, a sign of mutual respect between a villain and a police dog in a civilian setting.

Yet this slight anxiety of seeing Diabolo is quickly forgotten by the punters in The Six Bells when the blissful-looking Gilberto in his cap strolls in, smiling and waving. Many of them cheer, whilst others shout out: 'Great hat.'

Then the whole pub erupts when Carlotta arrives as, for a second, they think it is Marilyn Monroe. Yet despite her not being Marilyn, her beauty and natural charm oozes through the air. Well, after all, she is a good witch with a kind heart.

'Mario, your family and friends are welcome in Foxham,' declares Charles, which receives more loud cheers.

Soon, everyone is the best of friends. Chester, along with the Cambridges— well, apart from Owen—are talking to Gilberto. Diabolo and Sergeant Ali are getting on like long-lost friends and, to overcome the language barrier, the two dogs are speaking in Woof. Mario is talking to Boris. Silvia is in deep conversation with Anna and Sebastian. George is sharing a joke with Reggie. Betty is having a good natter with Kaye.

Owen, Bernard, Hector, Arnold, Henry, Isabella and Charlie are in the snug bar, talking amongst themselves and to Alberto, who jumps for joy when he spots the pizzas. As the jolly fox runs to help himself to a slice of pizza, he shouts out, 'Gilberto, pizzas!' Alberto's booming voice draws the attention of Carlotta, who is mingling with a lot of the villagers. Carlotta quickly walks to the snug bar just to make sure Alberto does not eat all the pizzas.

Trudi has her eye on Alberto, as she knew the moment he walked through the door of The Six Bells that he is a greedy fox.

Trudi looks straight away at Carlotta as she enters the snug bar. Carlotta sees her, nods and smiles—there is a bond between them straight away. Carlotta discreetly points at Alberto and mouths the words, 'I will protect him, but you have to save him.' Trudi now knows her destiny has finally arrived.

14

The Eve of Ruin

'I am sorry, but the gate has now closed. The next available flight to London Heathrow is tomorrow morning at 08.00. I am pleased to say that there are two seats available in smoking. Would you like me to book these seats for you, sir?' declares Luigi, the pleasant ticket clerk fox at the Alitalia desk, to Ettore in his new straw trilby hat, which was purchased in the airport gift shop to replace his damaged musketeer hat.

Ettore, upon hearing there are no flights until tomorrow, is now fearing the wrath of Enoch, for the cat assured his master that they would not miss their flight after the minor car accident. Enoch, believing the words of a cat who has never travelled outside of Italy before, decided to have a grilled prosciutto and fontina cheese sandwich with a cold glass of beer in Giovanni's bar, next to the airport, while Ettore went to purchase their flight tickets, leaving the luggage with Enoch.

Clutching his straw trilby hat in his left paw, Ettore, with concern, gently pulls the glass door of Giovanni's bar open with his right paw. Ettore's anxiety turns to delight upon seeing a merry Enoch in his favourite purple suit and white frilly shirt, with his arms around two tough working men from the streets of Naples, who have probably finished their shift at the airport and are now having a well-deserved beer.

The inebriated Enoch yells out, 'Giovanni! Drinks for my new friends and for those bears.' Ettore sees a family of bears in their Sunday best—a mother, a father and two cubs, a boy and a girl—sitting at a white-clothed table on metal-framed chairs with plastic red stripe seating, directly opposite from Enoch and the workmen. The father bear just nods to Enoch, whilst the mother bear pulls her two cubs closer to her.

Ettore, chuckles, whispering to himself, 'Just like the witches, he can't hold his drink.' Now Ettore knows this is as good a time as any to tell Enoch that they have missed their flight.

'Ettore, have a beer, you mischievous cat,' says Enoch as he turns to see the smiling cat at the bar's entrance. As Ettore makes his way to the bar, the two workmen get up and walk over to the pinball machine in the corner. Both men shake the father bear's paw, nod to the mother bear and smile to the cubs, as they stroll past.

'Ettore, hic, you're my best friend ever,' slurs Enoch.

'Thank you, master. Master?'

'Yes, best friend?'

'We can't get a flight until tomorrow.'

Enoch looks at Ettore with amazement then says, 'What?' in a sober manner.

'We have missed our flight, master. Would you like another beer?' says Ettore, hoping to defuse the situation.

Enoch, like a portrait painting, does not move a muscle, as he absorbs the bad news, but then like Mount Vesuvius, Enoch erupts. 'Get out, you nasty cat.' Ettore goes to sip his beer before departing, but Enoch snatches the glass from his paw. 'No beer for you. No beer for anyone. No more beer.' Then Enoch slumps his head into his arms, as he starts to sob. Ettore goes to his master to comfort him in his hour of need.

■ ■ ■

'We are going to have some fun in London,' says Monica to the coven in her hotel room at Claridge's, Mayfair. All the witches, now looking like beautiful and stylish models who could grace any catwalk in the world, nod and cackle in agreement. 'I can feel the evil surfacing,' continues Monica, now feeling a sense of worth, after her turbulent return to lead the Witches of Benevento.

■ ■ ■

Unlike Ettore and Enoch, the Witches of Benevento managed to catch their flight from Naples to Heathrow. Andriana blew some rose petals upon boarding the plane, as she recited an ancient spell to enchant all the passengers and crew. Andriana's spell worked wonders, as everyone wanted to be their friends.

Upon landing, the witches got through Arrivals without any incident. In fact, all the customs officers bent over backwards to assist them.

Two day prowlers, Norris Morris and Brian Rose, who the witches have prearranged to meet and drive them to London from Heathrow, linger outside the airport like they are waiting for some big Hollywood film stars.

After the brief and formal meet and greet, Morris in his black Humber Hawk with Monica and Caterina, Rose in his light blue Vauxhall Victor with Diana, Andriana and Benedetta, drive the five witches to their luxury hotel in Mayfair, London, because for the witches, money is no object. Prior to leaving Naples, at the villa near Castello e Torre di Montesarchio, Enoch gave Monica and Diana a list of sinful and wealthy benefactors in England who dabble in dark rituals and believe the best fox is the one being hunted and will be more than willing to assist the witches financially or suchlike.

Just before the witches and the day prowlers set off from Heathrow to Mayfair, Morris and Rose are given strict instructions by Monica not to converse with them any more. For you see, witches have a low opinion of day prowlers, as they can't abide how they creep around them.

Monica and Caterina step out of the black Humber Hawk, with Morris, holding the passenger door open for them. Both witches breathe in the cold evening air, as Morris hands over a beaten brown leather medical bag. Within the bag, is a £1000 cash donation from Dr Geoff Hunt, who booked and paid for the witches to stay at Claridge's, Mayfair,

But Morris did not expect the fast and powerful stomach punch from Caterina, as her mother snatches the bag from him. Monica gazes at the winded and slightly hunched-over Morris with every ounce of malevolence in her soul—which is a lot—before whispering in a cold and harsh voice, 'Foolish man, aren't you going to thank my daughter?'

Morris, now in fear for his safety, anxiously replies, 'Thank you, Madame Caterina.' Caterina giggles in a fiendish manner, before punching Morris in the stomach again. This time, Morris, in more pain, doesn't need any prompting from Monica. 'Thank you, Madame Caterina.'

'Now, be gone human, before I turn you into a toad. Be gone, I say,' orders Monica in a demonic voice. Morris cannot get into his car fast enough, as the idea of being a toad certainly doesn't appeal to him.

As Morris spins off in his black Humber Hawk into the streets of London, Caterina with wicked glee says, 'Look, mother! Diana, Andriana and Benedetta are beating up the other day prowler!'

Monica looks over and, to her amusement, sees that Andriana has Rose in a headlock, whilst Diana and Benedetta take turns to punch him in the face. Rose screams out in pain and terror, with each blow.

'Those silly humans that help us do not know that they will be our slaves when we conquer Earth,' states Monica, before heading into the Claridge's lobby.

■ ■ ■

'Thank you, Reggie. I know you will love my grandmother's beef cannelloni,' says Trudi at the counter of Milano's.

'Thank you, Trudi. Before you and your gran moved to Foxham and Blades got arrested, I didn't like all this foreign muck. But now, I love it. But I am sorry to say it is Ferdy's fish and chips on a Friday night for me tea,' replies the elderly customer.

'Ha! Well, as long as every other day is for Milano's, then I am more than happy,' jokes Trudi, as she tries her best to disguise her dislike for Ferdy, who still hasn't paid any tax.

'Before I forget, could I have a few slices of your Italian lemon cake? It's to go with me three o'clock cup of tea. And a few slices of that ricotta and sausage pie, please? Me pension comes on Thursday—can I settle up with you then?' enquires Reggie, with a new love for Italian food. Well, apart from Friday's, when it is fish and chips.

'Of course you can, Reggie. Here's four slices of each, but only pay us for two of each on Thursday,' says Anna, who along with Carlotta, has come from the back room of Milano's to talk to Trudi.

'Hello, Madame Anna, Miss Carlotta. Thank you. I'll see you on Thursday,' says Reggie, as he heads for the door.

'Bye, Reggie. Please be a darling and put the "Back in 15 minutes" sign up on the way out,' says Carlotta. Reggie is only too happy to oblige.

Within two minutes, Carlotta, Anna and Trudi are in the flat above Milano's. 'Thanks to Gilberto introducing us to his London crow friends, one of them just flew to tell me that he has seen the witches in a hotel in Mayfair, London,' says a serious Carlotta.

'Mayfair? Is that in London then?' asks Trudi.

'Yes, it is,' replies Carlotta.

'Oh, I thought it was just some place on the Monopoly board,' says Trudi, now feeling a little bit stupid.

Carlotta sweetly smiles at her fellow witches, then resumes her serious role. 'The coven won't do anything for a while. But I will speak to Charles this week. We must warn him.'

'He already knows that something is wrong. Many centuries ago, his ancestors were close to the good witches of the woods. A strong bloodline like that is never broken, it just lays dormant. Even though for Charles to practise magic would take forever, he still does have the mind's eye. I could sense it, the very evening you came to The Six Bells,' reveals Anna.

'Good. Then it won't be a shock when I tell him that five witches—as I had a vision that Monica has returned from the dead—are planning a deadly attack on Foxham. But we can't put fear into this village, not yet,' declares Carlotta.

'What about Alberto? Is he safe?' asks Trudi, who in the past few days has been going into Foxham Woods to be at one with nature and to develop the good magic within her soul.

'Yes, they are all safe at Fox Hill Hall. Charles has given him, Mario and Silvia the whole of the west wing. Gilberto couldn't be happier with the Campbells—saw him this morning, helping out Betty in the garden—and I love living with you two,' says Carlotta, who has never felt happier than living in Anna's large flat above Milano's. Trudi moved out of the cottage next to the care home and into Anna's flat, as the three of them wanted to be together.

Trudi's move proved fortuitous for Chester, as the fox now lives in the cottage next to the care home, which he shares with Diabolo, and as Diabolo's English improves, their friendship blooms.

'Thank you, my dear, and we love living with you,' replies Anna in a happy mood.

'No!' screams Trudi.

'What is it, Trudi?' asks a concerned Anna.

'I have just thought: as Charles has magic in his bloodline, that means Charlie does, too. He will turn against us, for he is a nasty little fox,' cries Trudi.

'Trudi, Charlie is a naughty fox, but he is just young and foolish. But you know as well as I do, deep down he is a good fox,' says Carlotta.

'It must be a bottomless pit to find a good soul in that fox. Well, only the other day I caught him and the poor misled Owen trying to steal milk from the milk cart. I knew it was all a pretence that Charlie had turned over a new leaf,' snaps Trudi, who finds it impossible to like him.

'Yes, that Owen is a sweet little fox. Shame he has Charlie for his best friend,' says Anna in agreement.

'Ha, I think you will find that Owen is just as naughty as Charlie. Anyway, that is not the issue. I can feel evil growing, so we must prepare for the battle,' says a confident yet slightly nervous Carlotta, with Anna and Trudi nodding in agreement.

■ ■ ■

3.33am: the full moon beams down on a ruined church on the outskirts of London, with five hideous witches, one menacing, yet well-dressed dark lord, an assortment of fiendish ghouls and three day prowlers transfixed by a cat in a bowler hat, bought from Harrods that afternoon, dancing on a broken stone altar.

'Dance, Ettore! Dance to the moon! Dance to the night! Dance, cat! Dance!' declares Enoch, as he gulps red wine from a golden goblet. All the ghouls wail, the day prowlers clap their hands and the witches—now all dressed in black and in their true wrinkled skin, pointed noses with long grey hair—cackle, as a pretence that they are relishing the dancing cat.

Monica is especially upset, as it was the tradition that she was the one who danced on the Eve of Ruin Carnival, a festivity held in the early hours of the morning at a fallen place of worship to celebrate the beginning of an evil crusade of horrendous suffering before the demise of their foes. Yet Enoch insisted the honour of doing the dance belonged to the new second in command, Ettore. As Ettore dances away, Enoch savours the thought of invading Foxham, witnessing the sacrifice of Alberto in front of the traitor Carlotta and executing 'i sogni dei bambini'.

■ ■ ■

The dark lord and the black cat managed to board a flight to Heathrow two days after missing their original flight, for Enoch had a terrible hangover and was ill after his drinking session at Giovanni's Bar next to Naples International Airport.

Unlike the Witches of Benevento, who were adored on their flight to England, Enoch and Ettore received no preferential treatment from the air hostesses, and the other passengers were weary and, at times, rude to these two servants of sin.

After landing and both swearing revenge on everyone on that flight, Enoch and Ettore had a great deal of difficulty at Passport Control, as an officer thought that Ettore looked nothing like his passport photo. But Ettore pointed out to the officer that he had put on weight since that photo had been taken. So, after an hour or so of questioning, the wicked duo could enter England.

Enoch and Ettore were greeted in Arrivals by a day prowler, Dawn Evans, a schoolteacher who hates children, to drive them to Claridge's, Mayfair, as on the morning of their flight, Enoch telephoned Dr Geoff Hunt, who informed Enoch where the witches were staying.

As Dawn Evans dropped Enoch and Ettore at Claridge's, they thanked her for her services, as neither could be bothered to be cruel to her, as they were saving their anger for the witches who were living the high life in London.

Moreover, when Enoch and Ettore arrived at Claridge's, the dastardly duo were annoyed to see that the witches were staying in the best rooms, with all the staff treating them like royalty and the other hotel residents adoring them. The witches were shocked to see Enoch and Ettore, as they had no idea they would be coming over to England.

That very evening, Enoch relocated the witches to two standard double rooms, with Monica and Caterina sharing one room, Diana, Andriana, and Benedetta the other.

Meanwhile, Enoch and Ettore took over the best suite in the hotel—the witches were not best pleased. Their annoyance was heightened further when Enoch announced upon arrival that Ettore is his second in command. That very evening, Monica went to the hotel bar to drown her sorrows, which only took three small glasses of wine.

■ ■ ■

Anna Milanese was right—Charles Reynard knew that Mario's surprise visit to the village was not a spontaneous holiday. Being a wise fox and one born into magic, Charles sensed that Mario and his entourage had fled to Foxham as they were in danger—and, more importantly, to save the world.

Therefore, when Carlotta, along with Trudi and Anna, tells Charles in his study the situation, he merely replies, 'I have known about the prophecy since cubhood and was aware that it may happen during my lifetime. When I took over this place, I found the ancient manuscript and the bottle of liquid magic from Barbagia, Sardinia, in the library, which are locked away in my safe upstairs. Only those that arrived from Naples know about this?'

'Well, we did survive it,' jokes Carlotta.

Charles, sitting on his velvet chair in his all-burgundy attire of plus fours, satin smoking jacket and smoking cap, smiles, sips his brandy, then says, 'Good. Make sure they keep quiet until we have a solid plan.'

'I don't think we will have any problems there, as they all seem to be enjoying themselves. Alberto is good friends with your grandson Charlie,' says Carlotta, which makes Trudi shudder as the mere mention of Charlie's name makes her tremble.

'Are you unwell, Trudi?' asks Charles upon seeing her discomfort. Trudi, realising what she has done, replies, 'Just a little bit of a cold, but I am fine, thank you for asking, Charles.'

Carlotta, away from Charles' observation, smiles at Trudi, as she knows the real reason for her shiver. Then Carlotta picks up the conversation. 'Mario and Silvia are enjoying their strolls around Foxham, Gilberto is loved by everyone, and Diabolo is...'

'...Chester's best friend. They are always laughing and joking. Diabolo's English is getting better,' cuts in an excited Trudi, trying to take her mind off Charlie.

'That is good news and we must make sure the whole village stays happy. If the

143

villagers find out about the witches now, they will become scared and will be weak when they face evil. So, mum's the word,' declares Charles.

■ ■ ■

For a few months, Foxham has been a happy place to live, from the building of the train station to the young members of the village playing on the common at the weekends. Most of the good folk of this place are none the wiser about the evil that is approaching.

However, once a week at the study in Fox Hill Hall, Charles, Carlotta, Trudi, Anna and Mario meet to discuss their tactics, as well as offer each other moral support. Charles, who was deeply involved with the planning of D-Day, decides to move from being cautious to protective.

'Tomorrow is the first of April, so we will send Gilberto to get a message to your men and foxes, Mario, and the bears of Campania that they are needed here. The witches will have spies at the airports, train stations and seaports. These evil creatures are listening to our telephone calls and reading our letters. I can sense it.'

Carlotta and Trudi, who have been growing in confidence and in magic, both reply, 'They are getting closer.'

Charles nods and says, 'Yes, they are. But we will beat them. I know we will. Gilberto is our best and only chance to get our message to Italy, so those fearless and strong reinforcements will arrive, ready for battle. But until they get here, it's business as usual in Foxham.'

■ ■ ■

But the following morning, after Gilberto set off to Italy, the expected food deliveries for Foxham from the nearby farms did not arrive. Moreover, by midday, the telephone poles caught fire, and by late afternoon, many of the villagers came down with a terrible cold.

So, in the early evening, Carlotta along with Trudi, Charles, Mario and Diabolo, with Boris as the chauffeur, drove Charles' Bentley out of Foxham Hill Hall and onto the main road out of the village to find food and medicine.

■ ■ ■

The crammed Bentley comes to an abrupt halt, as the car gently crashes into thin air. Fortunately for the passengers, Boris always drives just under the speed limit. Had Boris been driving like a maniac, similar to Diabolo around Naples, then this could have easily been a fatal accident.

'I am sorry, everyone. I have no idea what happened. There is nothing on the road. Is anyone hurt?' asks Boris, concerned yet annoyed that he has crashed Charles' beloved Bentley for no reason.

Carlotta opens the left passenger door and steps out of the Bentley. Charles, Trudi, Mario, Diabolo and Boris get out of the car, and decide to follow her.

Carlotta slowly walks with both of her arms in front of her. Then like the car's peculiar accident, Carlotta comes to a sudden stop.

Carlotta turns to her friends, who are standing only a few feet behind her, and says with unease, 'The witches have put a false field around Foxham. We are going to starve to death or die from a fever. I hope Gilberto makes it to Naples.'

As Carlotta ends her sentence, the sound of a witch's cackle pierces the evening sky.

15

The Siege of Foxham–Milano's

'My crops are ruined,' cries out Todd Meadows, a hardworking fox farmer known throughout Norfolk for his sense of humour and generosity. But today, Todd Meadows is not laughing—the first time in 10 years he has not.

Three days ago, Todd employed Yallery Brown, the mischievous spirit from Lancashire, as a labourer at his farm near Foxham.

Yallery Brown turned up at Todd's farm in a battered black sack suit, with a broad-brimmed black felt hat with his long blond scruffy hair sticking out, in beaten-up, black hobnail boots.

Brown, with crocodile tears, declared to Todd that he was famished and destitute. The kind-hearted Todd gave the wandering spirit a job, along with bed and board. But Todd's act of kindness was rewarded by an act of cruelty, as Brown intentionally damaged all his crops.

After trashing Todd Meadows' livelihood, Yallery Brown stole his bike and rode it to Hickling Broad marsh, five miles from Foxham, to meet the ghouls, goblins, banshees, a handful of cyclops from Great Britain and the fierce black ghostly dog Black Shuck from Norfolk, who were gathering here in secret.

Some of these wicked beings have been in hibernation since the 15th Century, therefore becoming part of British Folklore. Yet some, like Yallery Brown and Black Shuck, have been causing mayhem and mischief across the land when they can.

Yallery Brown and the other fierce creatures, dormant or not, felt compelled to go to Hickling Broad marsh after receiving a vision that a dark lord, a black cat, and five witches would be coming to Norfolk to lead an evil army. Yet their premonition

came about from a strong telepathic spell cast by the Witches of Benevento, from the comfort of Claridge's, Mayfair.

■ ■ ■

In Foxham Hill Hall's study stand a deflated Charles, Mario, Diabolo, Boris, Trudi and Carlotta. After Boris crashed the Bentley into a false field surrounding the village, they wandered through Foxham back to Reynard's residence, jaded and in shock.

Charles tries to raise their spirits. 'Foxham won't die from the fever or starve to death.'

Carlotta replies with reluctance, 'Charles, the witches are getting stronger by the day and I can feel their allies nearby. They are going to try everything they can to plunge this world into darkness.'

'Are you saying we are doomed?' asks a sad Boris.

'No, we are not,' cries out Diabolo in perfect English, the tough Doberman from Albania who survived the cruel sea.

'There might be more of them, yet we are smarter and our bond is stronger,' delivers a determined Trudi.

Suddenly, there is a loud banging on the oak front door of Foxham Hill Hall. 'It is George. I will let him in,' says Carlotta, seeing him in her mind's eye.

'No, allow me,' says Boris, leaving the study to greet George.

Within two minutes, George is standing in the study. With concern and some fear, he says, 'All my workers are ill. I see no food was delivered today. And half an hour ago, I tried to leave the village to see what has happened, but I crashed into something, I don't know what. Please, Charles, what is going on?'

'Let us go into the sitting room and I will explain,' reveals Charles.

■ ■ ■

Mario, Diabolo and George sit on a carved mahogany and gilt sofa in the far side of the sitting room. Trudi and Carlotta sit opposite on the same design of sofa. Boris decides to stand by the oak door, with Charles sitting in an upright mahogany and gilt chair in the middle, pulled slightly back from the sofas.

'Hello,' says Kaye, as she opens the sitting-room door, knocking Boris slightly.

'Hello, Kaye,' everyone replies.

'I am going into the kitchen. I'll do a nice round of chicken sandwiches, with some pork pies and crisps. It will have to be lemonade to drink, as Ferdy is in, and if he sees beer being drunk… well, you know what will happen,' exclaims Kaye, who is aware of the evil approaching Foxham.

'Madame Kaye, please allow me,' requests Boris.

'No, Boris, you are needed here. I will get Charlie to help me.' The moment Kaye says the name Charlie, both Charles and Carlotta look at Trudi, who is trying her best not to show her anger.

'Thank you, Kaye,' says George, who is anxious to hear what Charles has to say.

Then Ferdy, in a purple striped boating blazer, white trousers, a white Lacoste polo shirt and a straw boating hat, walks past his mother and into the sitting room.

'Ferdy, there is no gambling or drinking here. We are having a meeting,' shouts Charles to his unruly son.

'Yes, father, I know, and I have known all the time about the Witches of Benevento,' snaps Ferdy.

'Oh, earwigging again. Ferdy, you are my son and I love you, but please go. There is no scam here,' pleads Charles.

'Father, we are of the same bloodline—foxes that walked side by side with the good witches of the woods many centuries ago. We were at peace, until the bad witches and warlocks sided with the rich and hunted us across our fields and woods, as they knew if they broke our beautiful alliance, then they would become stronger,' says Ferdy in a stern manner.

For Carlotta, this is the first time she has heard Ferdy speak from the heart.

'Witches? Warlocks? I don't understand,' exclaims George.

'Ferdy, I hear you, but please, first, I must tell George everything,' says Charles, with Ferdy nodding his head in agreement.

■ ■ ■

'Soon, my wicked friends, very soon, we will sacrifice that ugly fat fox…' announces Enoch in a noble manner, as he stands on a makeshift timber platform in the middle of Hickling Broad marsh, with Ettore on his right-hand side, and Diana, Monica, Caterina, Andriana and Benedetta just standing behind the dark lord and the black cat in a bowler hat.

As Enoch exclaims the words 'ugly fat fox', the sinful crowd erupts into euphoria, bellowing at full volume with voices from the world of nightmares, 'Kill the fat fox! Kill the fat fox! Kill the fat fox.'

■ ■ ■

Enoch and his entourage arrived an hour ago at Hickling Broad marsh from London, after receiving lifts from the day prowlers Norris Morris, Brian Rose and Dawn Evans, to a hero's reception. Enoch allowed Dawn Evans to leave this unsavoury gathering unscathed, but Norris Morris and Brian Rose are less fortunate, as they are now at the mercy of Yallery Brown and Black Shuck.

The screams of pain from these day prowlers delight the evil crowd, and the other day prowlers, who are foolish enough to attend this immoral rally, now know it is only a matter of an hour or so before they, too, are the poor victims of Yallery Brown and Black Shuck. For you see, dear readers, the life of a day prowler is that of misery.

■ ■ ■

'Betty, that is why Carlotta and her friends came to Foxham. She and Charles told me everything, but we can't tell Bernard,' whispers George to Betty in their kitchen, hoping not to disturb their son as he sleeps. Yet their plan is useless, as the cries from the marshland five miles away awake Bernard.

'Mummy, daddy, what is that noise?' asks Bernard, coming down the stairs.

'Nothing, sweetheart, just some fools on the marsh. I will make you a nice, hot drink and some toast. I'll bring them up to you. Go back to bed. I will be up in a minute,' says Betty, hoping her son isn't too scared.

'Mummy, I am missing Gilberto. Is he coming home?' asks the sleepy child.

'Yes, dear,' assures Betty.

'Of course, he is—he's your best friend and best friends always come back,' guarantees George to his son, whilst glancing at Betty. George, like Diabolo is fearless and strong, and he will not let Foxham go down without a fight.

■ ■ ■

'I haven't heard anything from Gilberto,' says Carlotta to Anna and Trudi, in the front room of the flat above Milano's in the early hours of the morning. Yet it is not all dismay for these witches, as Trudi has just created a potion that will bring the fever to an end that has been spreading throughout Foxham. 'The fever is a weak spell. Very weak. I don't think those witches believed that I was strong enough to find a cure.'

'Well done, Trudi. Charles has called an emergency meeting at midday today in the centre of Foxham Common. But I think now everyone knows something is rotten, as they know they cannot leave Foxham and I am sure everyone has been woken from the ghastly cries from the marshes,' states Anna.

'The witches think the screams, the fever and the starvation will divide Foxham, making their invasion easier. So, it is up to us to keep this village united,' reflects Carlotta. Anna and Trudi nod in agreement.

■ ■ ■

Ferdy, sober for a change, sits in his small study in the south wing of Fox Hill Hall, whilst the rest of the household are in the main kitchen, after hearing the evil wailing from Hickling Broad marsh.

Ferdy is studying an old map of Foxham from when it was Stoke Ham Village and an ancient astrological chart that he found in the attic this afternoon. Then out of nowhere, Ferdy starts to speak in Latin, a language he hasn't used since he left school. Yet the magic in this fox's soul is coming to the forefront, as Ferdy can now see how to create a portal for a short period of time in the false field surrounding Foxham.

■ ■ ■

Oliver and Thomas sit in their front room, whilst Victoria is comforting Owen in his bed, after the Cambridges heard the blood-curdling screams from Hickling Broad marsh. Charles told his good friend Oliver, last week in confidence, about the witches and the prophecy.

Oliver, aware that Foxham is now under siege, has turned to his son Thomas, an avid reader, and a keen amateur historian, for much-needed advice on military-type blockades and preventing an evil prophecy.

Yet Thomas is fretting, as most of the sieges he is reading about, be it Megiddo or Carthage, succumbed to the invaders. Then, by accident, Thomas reads about the Battle of Faesulae when those under siege beat the intruders.

'Father, the witches and their army will march in and try and slaughter us in our homes. Some may even welcome them, thinking they are saviours that can cure the fever and the famine,' declares Thomas.

'Thomas, dear cub, no one will welcome these evil beings. Many of us, including me, fought the Nazis, so we know about the threat of invasion. I just always hoped

I would never have to participate in a war again. Young British folk against young German folk—all wrong,' says Oliver, as he wipes away a tear.

Thomas, seeing the sadness in his father, decides to discuss tactics, so Oliver can focus on the immediate danger.

'Father, what we must do is to stop this evil army from getting to the turret of the old medieval tower on Foxham Common. We can lay traps in the way, for delaying them is our best weapon, so Trudi can fulfil the good prophecy. From my studies, I think witches and other evil forces do not like iron. So, if we had some iron… then we could build a barrier.'

Oliver wishes his three brothers were here: Jeffrey, who now lives in France and is in the aeronautical industry, and Harold and Cropper, who both live in Hackney and work for the council. Before Oliver had learned about the witches, he had sent letters to all three of them, telling his brothers how wonderful life is in Foxham. Right now, though, Oliver needs their help, but with the telephone lines down and a false field around the village, this is an impossible request.

'Father, are you listening? We need iron,' says Thomas to his father, as he can see he is distracted.

'Iron, you say, Thomas?'

'Yes, father. Iron.'

'Then we will go and see George, for there is plenty of steel being used for the train station. Steel has a great deal of iron. Come on, Thomas. Let us dash to our neighbours.'

The Campbells and the Cambridges live within a five-minute walk of each other and are good friends, often going to each other's houses for dinner, where Owen and Bernard play games along with Gilberto, whilst Thomas talks to the adults, as he is awkward around anyone in his age group. In fact, Thomas is often teased for his love of books, especially by Charlie. But right now, Thomas' studious ways may have propelled him into becoming a hero.

∎ ∎ ∎

Stefano Romano, the handsome pilot, sits at the end of an old and large conference table in a slightly run-down office in the historical city centre of Naples. Giorgio, Giuseppe and Giovanni Colombo; the boxing wolves from Benevento, Francesco and Leonardo; an array of Mario's gang; and some pilots are seated on either side of the table.

Since Stefano was apprehended by the wolves a while back at a disused airport in Naples after refusing to fly the witches of Benevento to England, he has joined the good fight. Stefano has brought in pilot friends who, in turn, have helped to keep the red-capped goblins at bay, resulting in Eder and Edor fleeing Italy to England. Yet this collection of good souls knows that something bad is brewing.

'Since yesterday morning, we have not been able to speak to Mario—the lines of communication to Foxham are down,' says Franco, a human henchman for Mario.

Stefano, who has quickly emerged as one of the leaders of this group, looks at his new and old friends. One is Jeffrey Cambridge, Oliver's brother, who now runs a small private airfield in Marseille, France. Stefano and Jeffrey became good friends, as the Italian often takes off and lands at the fox's airfield.

'I picked up a letter only yesterday from my brother Oliver in Foxham, after I went back to Marseille to pick up some new socks. He says that everything is great—my brother would tell me if he was in danger. I plan to fly to Norfolk after Easter for a little surprise. I have bought a book about the Roman Empire for my nephew Thomas and a catapult for my other nephew Owen,' says Jeffrey.

However, Jeffrey, his friends and the rest of the world may be living in Hell on Earth on Easter Monday.

■ ■ ■

Gilberto, sweating and trembling, is confused, for after he flew from Foxham to Italy to find reinforcements, Diana sensed that Gilberto was leaving England, so the wicked witch cast a spell from London on Gilberto for him to literally get lost in the sky.

So now Gilberto is in Oslo, Norway, miles away from Italy.

The crow starts to weep, fearing that he has failed his new friends. Then hope is slightly restored when Gilberto sees a male fox and a female fox walking through the city, both sharply dressed in their evening attire, with the male fox resembling Otto, a fox that Gilberto has found to be friendly in Foxham.

'Dear sir and madam,' Gilberto squeaks as the foxes walk past. The fox couple turn to see a distressed crow, then the male fox starts to lick his lips like a hungry fox…

■ ■ ■

Eder and Edor terrorised the Chevrolets, a family of humans from France, to take them all the way on their sailing boat, from the Bay of Naples to Great Yarmouth. The Chevrolets, until they met the red-capped goblins, were having a lovely holiday around the coastlines of Italy.

When Eder and Edor hatched a plan to flee the region of Campania, they telephoned Enoch at Claridge's, Mayfair, from the villa near the Castello e Torre di Montesarchio, for the dark lord had told them of his movements and both goblins had mastered the art of using the phone. However, Enoch knew two red-capped goblins arriving in a prestigious part of London would draw unnecessary attention to him and the witches, so he told Eder and Edor to go to Great Yarmouth, and he would arrange a day prowler or two to take them to Hickling Broad marsh, to congregate with the other evil beings that were starting to gather there.

The day prowlers jumped with fear when they saw two red-capped goblins clutching onto their battleaxes, stepping off the boat. The Chevrolets had aged 20 years, as their journey was like being at sea with the Devil. However, as this kind French family posed no threat to Eder and Edor, their lives were thankfully spared.

Fast-forward a week. Eder and Edor now stand in front of Enoch on Hickling Broad marsh, who brings the bloodthirsty crowd to order.

'Yes, we will kill the fat fox at the stroke of midnight on Easter Sunday. Now go and cause panic in the villages.' Enoch delivers his final sentence with such force that the whole wicked gathering goes into a frenzy. Yallery Brown dances and screams like a mad man, Black Shuck barks at the moon, Eder and Edor wield their axes towards the night sky as they grunt, the witches cackle, and Ettore meows, as he thinks of what hat to wear when they invade Foxham.

■ ■ ■

'Madam, I can assure you, there is no gathering of witches and ghoulies on the marsh, just some young folk being high spirited before Easter. Yes, madam… probably Teddy boys… yes, madam, I think Elvis should be in prison… thank you, madam… and good night… bloody thank you, madam, and good night,' says PC McDonald, a young policeman who so long wants to leave Norfolk and to be a policeman in London.

■ ■ ■

'I did it! There is a portal in the false field,' screams a happy Ferdy, in his black tuxedo, black trousers, white shirt and black bow tie. For this is the first time since Ferdy was a cub that he has done a good deed without trying to make a profit or pull off a scam, and he wanted to look good for this rare moment.

With Ferdy at the old medieval tower on Foxham Common are George, Charles, Oliver, Thomas, Trudi, Anna, Carlotta, Charlie, Diabolo and Chester, who was asked by his Doberman friend to come along.

'The portal will only last for about an hour. I haven't got time to explain the hows and whys; it's just down to the moving alignment of the stars. Now, let's go to

East London and get some backup,' says Ferdy, liking the role of a hero more than that of a swindler.

'I will come with you, Ferdy,' says Oliver.

'So will I,' remarks Diabolo, whose English is getting better by the day.

'Me, too,' says Chester.

'No, Chester. You have to look after the folk at the care home,' orders Trudi. Chester doesn't answer back, as Diabolo nods in agreement with Trudi.

'Father, I will join you,' says Thomas.

'No, Thomas, you are needed here, for you and George must help to build the traps and the steel wall around the tower. That is your job,' says Oliver.

'Yes, Thomas, I need you. You're the fox,' declares George.

'Father, I will join you,' says Charlie, which shocks everyone, especially Trudi.

'Charlie—your father, Diabolo and Oliver will be fine,' says Charles to his grandson.

'Grandfather, I know I have been a bad cub, done nothing but bring havoc to the village, but I love Foxham. Please, I want to go,' pleads Charlie sincerely.

Charles, a great admirer of bravery, puts his paws on Charlie's shoulders and says, 'You are a Reynard and I am proud of you.' And with those words, grandfather and grandson embrace.

George gets his notepad out of his overcoat pocket and quickly writes something down, tears the paper out of the pad and passes it to Ferdy, then says, 'These are the telephone numbers of my brothers and friends from Notting Hill. These boys can hold their own, so be sure to call them.'

Ferdy nods with confidence to George, then turns to his father and asks, 'When we come back and beat the witches, could you have a word with the tax inspector please?'

Charles doesn't say a word.

■ ■ ■

A few days later, early Easter Sunday evening, a foot steps onto Foxham High Road. It is Enoch and behind him is an army made from nightmares.

'Friends, Foxham is ours and by midnight, the world will be ours, too,' states the dark lord.

16

The Invasion of Foxham

Enoch, looking impeccable in a new tailor-made purple suit, red frilly shirt and black shining laced-up boots, all purchased from several shops in Jermyn Street, London, SW1, smiles a wicked smile as he gazes at the café, Milano's, then upon the green grass of Foxham Common and the oak trees of Foxham Woods, which loom over the greenery.

Along with the quaintness of the High Road, the common and the woods is Foxham Hill, a 10-minute stroll through the woods or 15 minutes if you turn right at the end of Foxham High Road. Upon this hill is the old medieval tower, an ancient relic that tonight will be instrumental in the destiny of the world. Moreover, in the roads and the lanes of Foxham and scattered around the Common are the homely houses and cottages, one pub (The Six Bells), and an array of shops and small boutiques. In addition, left of Foxham High Road is Fox Hill Lane, another hill, which leads to Fox Hill Hall, passing the Town Hall, the library, the court and the police station on the way.

By the dark lord's side stand his brutal bodyguards, the bloodthirsty red-capped goblins Edor and Eder, clutching onto their axes. At the back of Enoch and these vile creatures are Ettore the black cat in a new sailor's cap and the Witches of Benevento. All five witches refused Enoch's orders to stand behind Ettore as they entered Foxham. Enoch had further problems with the witches as he wanted them to look like aged hags for this evening, but the witches insisted they kept their attractive personas. Enoch was fighting a losing battle, so he has reluctantly succumbed to their demands.

Following Ettore and the Witches of Benevento are the mischievous and wicked Yallery Brown, the hound from hell, Black Shuck, and an army of 300 ghouls, goblins, banshees and a handful of cyclops. All the day prowlers were either too scared to join the invasion or they have—'cough, cough—'vanished.

The rest of this nasty militia are wandering around other villages of Norfolk, causing mayhem before they join the rest in Foxham.

■ ■ ■

Even though Enoch is looking forward to finally taking over the world, he is still annoyed that a famous vampire refused to help him.

Two weeks ago, from his suite at Claridge's, Mayfair, Enoch telephoned the famous vampire at his castle in Transylvania.

The famous vampire had Lupo, the leader of the werewolves, a lycanthrope who lost his human form many centuries ago, by his side when he answered the call from Enoch in the castle's library one Tuesday night.

Every Tuesday night, the famous vampire and Lupo get together for a game of cards, a few beers and many rounds of cheese on toast. Lupo is the first and only werewolf to go vegetarian, because after a hundred-odd years of eating nothing but raw red meat, Lupo started to get severe stomach cramp in 1928.

Nevertheless, Enoch did not expect the famous vampire and Lupo to mock him when he asked them to join his evil mission. 'Enoch, my dear friend, are you telling me that you are frightened of a village full of foxes?' asked the famous vampire when he heard Enoch's request, which made Lupo howl and laugh. Enoch, hurt and annoyed, slammed down the telephone's receiver and, as he did, he clipped Ettore round the ear.

■ ■ ■

Enoch, trying to forget about how the famous vampire and Lupo teased him, orders, 'Eder and Edor, take 50 of my army and charge across this filthy common. This will make the ill and the starving flee their homes in terror and into our arms.'

Enoch's words are adrenaline to the vicious duo of Eder and Edor, who raise their axes to the full moon as they lead an assortment of goblins, ghouls, banshees and one cyclops, along with Yallery Brown and Black Shuck, who howl and yell as they run with speed and power onto the green grass of Foxham Common.

As this loud and murderous army races across the common, watching from the oak trees of Foxham Wood are Thomas, George and a small army of foxes, badgers and humans clutching home-made bows and arrows.

'Argh!' is shrieked into the night air, as some of this army of nightmares falls into a 20-foot hole with wooden spikes, which has been covered by a roll of turf.

'Fire at will,' orders Officer Thomas, at which the dark sky is filled with a quiver of arrows. It was George who called Thomas 'Officer Thomas,' as George was impressed by Thomas' diligent knowledge of historical battles. Thomas, relishing the title officer, is donning his father's army uniform, which has been altered by his mother Victoria.

Enoch and his army thought the good folk of Foxham were all housebound, due to hunger or fever or both, for only the other night Diana was scrying the village from her 16th Century handheld Venetian mirror and saw a sleepy and afraid village. But this was an illusion created by Trudi and Carlotta, whose combined magical powers were able to intercept Diana's vision.

So, whilst Diana thought she was looking at a broken village on her mirror, George was using the hydraulic excavator from the building site for Foxham Railway Station to dig three large holes, 20 feet deep, on Foxham Common, the High Road and the lane leading to Fox Hill Hall. As George was busy making these booby traps, Mario used the Coles' diesel electric crane to lift all the steel tracks, so he could a build a wall of steel around the old medieval tower on Foxham Hill to keep out the witches and protect the other residents of the village, who will be there during the battle. George and Mario were, of course, helped by the other residents in their constructions, whilst Charles was sourcing any guns he could.

Those that were not assisting George and Mario went about other tasks. Some made bows, others made arrows, some tied household knives to broomsticks, whilst others sharpened the end of the broomsticks to make wooden spikes and a few rolled up turfs from gardens.

Klaus Fischer, a Rottweiler from Berlin and the village's blacksmith, who only moved to Foxham earlier this year for the building of the train station, worked non-stop, thanks to Anna making him frankfurters and sauerkraut, forging about 50 swords. Kaye, Betty and Silvia, along with the younger folk of Foxham, made sandwiches and pies, and stocked up on water for everyone on the battlefield and in the steel wall of the tower.

As Foxham had not received any food deliveries, Charles introduced brief rationing but stated everything would be fine come Easter Monday, and as you know, Trudi cast out the fever spell so Foxham is fighting fit.

■ ■ ■

'Charge!' orders Officer Thomas. The makeshift Foxham archery division throw down their bows and arrows in haste, as they pull out the swords made by Klaus

Fischer. Armed and raring to go, they charge towards the slightly depleted first platoon of Enoch's army, as Edor, Eder, Black Shuck, 20 or so goblins, ghouls and banshees plus one cyclops have fallen into the hole, leaving Yallery Brown to lead this division.

'Come on foxy, let's fight,' screams the roguish spirit.

Officer Thomas, inspired by the swashbuckling novels he has read, George influenced by the street fights of his younger days, and the foxes, badgers and humans, driven by the desire to save Foxham and the world, head on to Yallery Brown and his band of horrible souls with gritted teeth.

Yallery Brown fails to see Todd Meadows, the kind farmer who Brown ruined, creeping up to his right-hand side. Todd Meadows got into Foxham after Ferdy, Oliver and Diabolo found him walking towards the village after they left Foxham through the portal. Ferdy gave Todd directions to the portal and told him he had to hurry or it will be closed. When Todd arrived, Charles welcomed him with open arms.

Todd steps forward and plunges his sword into Yallery Brown's ribs. The blow is so powerful that it pushes Brown into the booby trap. Brown screams in pain as he lands on his side upon a sharpened broom handle. This delights Todd no end.

Enoch, seeing that the numbers are evenly matched in this battle, decides to put the odds in his favour. 'Disciples of evil, take your arms and no prisoners.'

Officer Thomas, after killing a banshee, looks up to see a group of hideous foot soldiers charging towards them, so he gives the order, 'Retreat! Retreat! There are too many of them.' The Foxham ensemble runs backwards, facing their enemy with their swords in their paws or hands.

The moment Officer Thomas and his army get a foot on the soil of the woodland, they all turn, run and split into two groups, with one going right, the other left, following painted signs on the trees, which only they know where to look for. Officer Thomas and George knew that one booby trap, an onslaught of arrows followed by a charge, would not see off Enoch and his army fully, but it would demoralise them.

Therefore, to destroy their confidence and slow them down further, Officer Thomas, along with Boris and Reggie, dug 10 smaller holes in the woods, with evil animal spring traps in them made by humans that had been confiscated by Charles over the years. Officer Thomas and Boris refused to touch the traps, so

Reggie, who has never hunted animals, with regret laid the traps, but he was reassured by his fox and badger friends that it was for a good cause.

As Officer Thomas and the rest of the gang run through the woods, all they can hear are the shrieks of goblins, ghouls and banshees falling into the nasty traps.

■ ■ ■

Enoch turns to Diana and says with much anger, 'The vision from your mirror of a village living in fear was a trick. I thought Carlotta and that fox witch were weak, but their spell has fooled you. Over the centuries, I have been involved in many sieges, but I have never seen a small army that is so well organised and so strong. And trust me, I hate saying that.'

Diana hangs her head in shame, as she can't believe that the beautiful and hip Carlotta and the last fox witch have got the better of her.

'I never knew that the fox witch would be so powerful,' says Benedetta. Like Diana, she, too, is surprised that their invasion hasn't gone according to plan.

'The Milanese's bloodline is the strongest one for magic in the foxes of Europe, but these foxes went into hiding when we started to hunt them, and when foxes learnt to talk, it seemed like the magic in their blood had vanished. Yet for some reason, in the one called Trudi, it has been reborn and stronger than before,' confirms Monica.

'Just make sure you keep that fox witch alive. For after we have fulfilled the prophecy, I want to drink the blood from her neck as she witnesses the rise of darkness,' declares Enoch.

'Just like Drac…' says Caterina, but she is cut short.

'Don't you dare say his name, for he is a fool and a traitor,' snaps Enoch.

'Well, you have no traitors here, Lord Enoch. Grimes, head of the Norfolk goblins, reporting for battle, master'

Enoch turns around to see a five-foot, broad and green-skinned goblin, dressed like a British red coat soldier from the 18th Century, but without the hat. Behind this goblin are 500, if not more, goblins dressed exactly like him, also without hats. Enoch smiles knowingly, believing now that Foxham will be no more within an hour.

■ ■ ■

The evening before the invasion, at a social club in Notting Hill, 'He's a good dancer and I love that suit,' Errol Campbell, George's younger brother, remarks to a drunken Oliver and Ferdy. Errol is, in fact, complimenting Diabolo on his tailor-made silver-grey suit and his fancy footwork on the social club's dance floor to Lord Kitchener's *Bebop Calypso*. For this evening, Diabolo has fallen in love with the sound of calypso, and the residents of Notting Hill, as the heart and soul of this district of London, remind Diabolo of his beloved Naples. The respect is not a one-way street, as the Campbell brothers and their friends adore Diabolo for his tough persona yet kind heart, and they quite like Oliver and Ferdy, too.

However, this Doberman and two foxes have got so caught up with the positive vibe of Notting Hill and due to one rum too many, they have forgotten the reason why they are here—and they haven't even got to East London yet.

■ ■ ■

'Throw over the ladders,' orders Officer Thomas, as he, George, Todd and the rest of Foxham's army run towards the old medieval tower, which is surrounded by layers of steel tracks. Upon hearing the words, Sergeant Ali, the retired Sergeant Brutus and PC Bryan throw three rope ladders made by Charlie, Owen, Henry, Isabella, Matthew Wright, Billy Wells and Bernard this morning over the barricade.

Mario, Foxy, Chester, Otto, Boris, Reggie and Charles stand on strong crates behind the steel wall, as they point their guns down the hill towards the approaching army of goblins, ghouls, banshees and two cyclops.

Charles was only able to find seven shotguns in the whole of Foxham, and three handguns from Mario—one apiece for Sergeant Ali, the retired Sergeant Brutus and PC Bryan—who will take their places on the crates, once officer Thomas and company are over the wall.

Officer Thomas, George and the rest of their troops have forgotten to take their bows and arrows with them after running back into the woods, and that was the plan. However, this is easier said than done, considering they are fighting to protect Foxham and the world.

This error is just about to prove costly for Officer Thomas. As he is climbing up the rope ladder, Greasy, a horrible goblin, bends down on his right knee to assume the archery position, takes aim and fires, from a bow and arrow he found in Foxham Woods.

The arrow flies up the hill and straight into Thomas' backside, who shrieks out in agony. Victoria, his mother, seeing her distressed son in pain as the top part of his body hangs over the steel wall, runs to his aid, and pulls brave Officer Thomas to safety.

'Fire,' orders Charles, upon seeing the arrow attack. The Foxham artillery division (Mario, Foxy, Chester, Otto, Boris, Reggie, Sergeant Ali, the retired Sergeant Brutus and PC Bryan, with Charles in command) obey without question. The bullets push Enoch's army slightly back into the woods, with the oak trees shielding them.

'Cease fire! We will only waste bullets,' orders Charles. The Foxham artillery division temporarily stop shooting.

■ ■ ■

Enoch, now wise to the booby traps, sends an unsuspecting team of 10 goblins from Grimes' troops ahead of the other foot soldiers. It does not take long for these evil green-skinned goblins to fall foul of a 20-foot trap in Foxham High Road. As the impaled goblins cry out for help, Enoch orders that no one is to help them, leaving them to die. No one cares about the goblins' suffering, apart from Ettore, who feels pity for them.

As Enoch's brutal army march, with 10 more green-skinned goblins ahead, through Foxham, the dark lord is disgusted with how beautiful the village is. So, he demands that some ghouls, goblins and banshees burn down as many houses as they can.

■ ■ ■

'Foxham is burning!' yells George, as he sees the flames and the smoke rising into the night's sky.

'Our beautiful home!' cries out Betty, coming out of the ground floor of the tower upon hearing her husband's concerned voice.

On the ground floor of the tower are the females, young folk, the foxes from the care home in their pyjamas, and the food and water supplies.

In the grounds of the tower, surrounded by the wall of steel, are the Foxham artillery division, ready for action, the male humans, and animals of the village, clutching home-made weapons or the swords forged by Klaus.

Klaus himself is guarding the entrance to the ground floor. The rottweiler is not there to protect the females, as they can look after themselves, but he has been instructed by Trudi to keep an eye on Charlie, for she caught the young rascal trying to steal some chicken sandwiches from the provisions.

When Trudi told Charlie off, he was his usual rude self, so she had a word with Klaus as she did not want to waste her magic on the cheeky fox. Klaus now has his beady eye on Charlie, who at this moment is behaving himself.

As for Trudi, she, Carlotta and Alberto are standing on the opposite side of Klaus by the entrance of the ground floor. All three stand in silence, with Alberto trembling slightly, for it is now 10.00pm and all three know in two hours' time, the world will either be saved or plummeted into darkness for eternity.

'Look! The army is getting bigger!' yells Chester.

'It is, too,' confirms Otto, as these two foxes look over the steel wall.

All the artillery division slowly put their guns down, to see more evil soldiers gathering in the woods.

'We need to keep them at bay for two more hours. We can do it. We are Foxham,' declares Charles.

'Of course we will, because this is my kind of fight. Oh boy, it's going to be fun,' says a rather delighted sounding Mario.

■ ■ ■

'Monica, we don't need to be waiting around in the woods with these horrible creatures. Let me call our broomsticks. I had the foresight to summon them here from Italy the other night. They are hovering outside, and all I have to do is whistle and I know how to whistle. We can grab that stupid cat as we fly into the night as real witches, not Enoch's stooges. For it is us who will sacrifice the fat fox,' whispers Diana to Monica, as the Witches of Benevento slowly follow the eerie army into Foxham Woods.

Monica holds her head high, and with both arms motions the Witches of Benevento to halt. Then the witch takes a deep breath and declares, 'Fellow witches, Diana speaks wise words. Let us fly into the night and fulfil the prophecy of "i sogni dei bambini". Just make sure Ettore, our one-time familiar, joins us.'

'Oh crikey,' says Ettore to himself upon hearing Monica's demand. So, the black cat in a sailor's cap tries to walk past the witches unnoticed. However, this proves fruitless for Ettore, as Andriana viciously picks him up from the ground and places the struggling cat under her left arm.

'Witches of Benevento, let us do some evil,' proclaims Monica, upon seeing Andriana's action. And with these words, the witches start to cackle, as they morph into their hideous and true selves.

■ ■ ■

'Cyclops, none of you have said a word—or more importantly done a thing—during this invasion. Now I order you to chop down these trees. Once the trees crash into the ground, you goblins, with your axes, are to cut off the branches, and you ghouls and banshees, with your swords, must shape the trees into battering rams to take that steel wall down, so we can get that horrible fat fox,' bellows Enoch.

Enoch's closing words, 'fat fox', sends the evil militia into a frenzy again as they shriek into the night's sky, 'Kill the fat fox! Kill the fat fox!'

Alberto, upon hearing the evil cry of 'kill the fat fox', by the entrance of the old medieval tower, turns to Carlotta, hugs her, then starts to cry. Carlotta hugs her friend back as she reassures him, 'Alberto, be strong. No one will harm you.'

Carlotta suddenly looks up to the night's sky and sees five witches on their broomsticks, flying towards the tower. 'Alberto, go and join your mother now. Go... Trudi, you and I have got some witches to fight,' says Carlotta, as she points to the sky so the witch fox can see their foes approaching.

Trudi responds to the situation by bravely stating, 'So, if it's a fight they want, then it's a fight they have got...'

17

The Battle of Foxham

As Trudi brings her declaration of war to a close, she, Carlotta, and the terrified Alberto, who disobeyed Carlotta to go with his mother, look up at the five hideous witches hovering above the steel wall surrounding the old medieval tower.

Fortunately for Foxham, the iron contained within the steel is preventing the witches from flying straight down into the yard so one of them can kidnap Alberto, with the remaining witches to cause pandemonium amongst the residents.

Nevertheless, their sheer grotesque presence in the moonlight sky makes all the young folk cry as they run to their mothers for protection. Seeing their fear delights Benedetta, who hollers so piercing and menacing in her best English, 'Little ones, enjoy your last hug with your mother because soon you will belong to us.' The nearby banshees are thrilled by this evil statement—so much so that they start to wail a horrid wail that makes the young folk, from Owen to Bernard, squeal in sheer terror.

Carlotta had thought and forewarned Trudi that the witches might try an airborne attack from their broomsticks. Therefore, she and Trudi, with some help from Anna, prepared several jar spells, magic spells and potions in jam jars, which are now in a battered brown leather doctor's bag by Alberto's feet, who is shaking so much that he is having trouble standing up.

Carlotta bends down, reaches into the bag and pulls out the jar spell of 'Flying Iron Filings'. Then the Marilyn Monroe lookalike takes aim and throws the jam jar directly at the nearest witch on a broom, Benedetta. Just before the jar smashes upon the wooden handle, Carlotta quickly looks up to the moon, and chants, 'Iron, ol zorge, eol unal enemies c mine nalvage,' then takes cover, pulling down Trudi as

she does, because they are both witches, therefore flying iron filings would weaken them, too.

Iron filings start to fill the air, which encircles the flying witches. Andriana, with the extremely nervous Ettore sitting on the brush of the flying broom, yells out in Italian, 'Go back! Go back!' Trudi starts to jump up and down with joy, yet for the folks of Foxham, their problems are far from over.

As Carlotta is seeing off the Witches of Benevento, the goblins, ghouls, banshees and a few cyclops, with the tree logs turned into battering rams, are smashing hard into the steel wall. The Foxham artillery division is shooting at this merciless collection of fiends. Yet these actions are proving futile—as one goblin or ghoul goes down, another one runs up the hill to take their place, so the ramming persists. George, Klaus and Officer Thomas, who is now back on his feet after his mother put a bandage on his backside, are standing as a three, holding their swords, ready for the invasion. 'Foxham, make a stand!' yells the brave George, like the rest of the village, male and female, human and animal, clutching onto swords and homemade weapons… Foxham will not go down without a fight.

Trudi, seeing the approaching danger, looks at her watch and says with much concern to Carlotta, 'I am not sure that we are strong enough to keep this army out.'

'Take young Alberto to the turret of the tower. Prepare. But you must believe that we will win.'

Trudi nods with some hesitation, because last year, her biggest concern was making sure Milano's had enough eggs, but this evening, her biggest concern is to save the world from darkness. There is a huge difference.

Diana and Benedetta, like Carlotta, Anna and Trudi, prepared some jar spells the night before the invasion. They fly towards the fiend army battering the steel wall and throw a jar each that contains grey smoke. As the jars smash onto the cold metal, they both chant, 'Quansb.'

There is an almighty explosion, which throws all the Foxham artillery division back into George, Klaus, Officer Thomas and their troops, making everyone fall over. All the mothers and young folk start to scream again.

Carlotta gets up, after being knocked down due to the blast, and looks at Trudi, who is hugging Alberto. 'They won't beat us. You know they won't,' says the good witch.

Diana and Benedetta's jar spell is so powerful, despite Monica telling them to make a mild bomb spell, that many of the goblins, ghouls and a few cyclops lay down on the ground, not moving. Moreover, the impact of the spell splintered the steel tracks, with many fragments flying into the air, which has thrown these two nasty witches off their broomsticks and onto the earth. The banshees, seeing this disaster, start to wail, then return to the war chant of 'Kill the fat fox! Kill the fat fox!' The war cry gives momentum to the goblins, ghouls and a few cyclops that are not involved in the battering of the wall made of steel.

Enoch, who is standing safely behind the oak trees of Foxham Woods, steps out into the darkness and yells to the night sky, 'Silence fiends, and listen.' All the goblins, ghouls, banshees and a few cyclops that aren't injured stop to listen to the dark lord, as do the two witches on the ground and the three witches flying above. 'We will honour those we have lost. Their weak wall has crumbled, nothing can stop us.

Our evil is strong, they are weak. Attack these fools, slaughter everyone, spare the fat fox, prepare for the sacrifice and the darkness… now go forth.'

And with that, a berserk army of nightmares charges towards the medieval tower with the broken steel wall.

'We can't hold them back! There are too many of them!' screams George upon seeing the approaching army, with Klaus and Officer Thomas by his side.

'We must hold them off—we have to!' yells Mario.

Then a shaking, thunder-like sound fills the air. The nightmare army stops to look up, as does the army of Foxham. Four planes, flying slowly just above the trees, comes into everyone's vision.

'My word, they are the USA C-130 Hercules planes,' says Officer Thomas.

'USA planes flying over England? Why?' asks Chester.

Then silhouette figures start to parachute out of three of the planes, with the other one descending towards the land, probably to land on marshland nearby. As the parachuting shadows glide down towards the battlefield, it becomes apparent that they are bears, foxes and a couple of wolves.

'It's back up from Naples!' yells a delighted and relieved Mario.

■ ■ ■

'Safe landing and good luck friends,' says Geoffrey, over his C-130 Hercules's tannoy system. Giorgio Colombo, leader of the bears of Campania, looks at Geoffrey Cambridge, who is piloting the plane. Geoffrey looks over his shoulder, sensing someone is staring at him. As he does, Giorgio salutes him. Geoffrey returns the gesture with pleasure.

Then Giorgio dives out of the plane and into the sky, the parachute opens, slightly pulling Giorgio back into the heavens, as he prepares for battle. His brothers Giuseppe and Giovanni, and more of the bears of Campania, follow their leader into the skirmish on Foxham Hill.

Stefano Romano wishes good luck to his parachute jumpers, which are foxes from Mario's gang in his C-130 Hercules, and in the other plane piloted by Marco Pecchia, a human and a close friend of Stefano, is a collection of bears, foxes, and Leonardo and Francesco the boxing wolves of Benevento, who along with Giorgio Colombo will lead the attack in Foxham.

Simone Libertazzi, a fox pilot, is landing his C-130 Hercules on Hickling Broad marsh. The wet ground is not ideal for landing, yet Simone is a highly skilled pilot, renowned for his touchdown skills. In this plane are the humans from Mario's gang and from this marshland they will make their way to Foxham by foot or car—that is, if they can steal one or two en route.

■ ■ ■

When Stefano Romano and his pilots, Leonardo, Francesco, the bears of Campania and Mario's gang learnt about the immediate danger that Foxham and the world are in— which you will discover how they found out shortly, I promise—Stefano, on behalf of the group, acted by going to his contacts at the USA airfield in Naples. He was able to source four C-130 Hercules aeroplanes; now he owes his American friends one huge favour.

Stefano didn't disclose the reason why he needed the planes.

Afterwards, at the Naples crew's crisis meeting, Giorgio Colombo decided that the bears would land by parachute in Foxham, saying that trying to land the air-crafts would take some planning and they would need permission from the British government to do so; this way they could fly into England undetected.

Leonardo and Francesco didn't want to be outdone by the bears, so they de-clared they would land by parachute, too, and the foxes from Mario's gang said they would do the same. However, the humans, thanks to the slight manipulation by the boxing wolf brothers of Benevento, favoured a more traditional landing.

If you have had the pleasure of having a holiday in Naples and her surrounding area, then you will notice it is not unusual to see a bear, a wolf or a fox rock climb-ing, hang-gliding or doing a parachute jump, as these animals love the thrill and excitement of these activities, whilst the humans of this area prefer to play football, basketball and baseball.

Stefano went back to his American friends to get some parachutes, so now he owes them two huge favours.

■ ■ ■

'Oh no!' screams Enoch, knowing full well that this orthodox parachute regiment is landing for his opponents. 'If only that silly vampire and that fool of a werewolf had helped, then it would be over by now,' Enoch says to himself.

'Look, it's the silly bears, some horrible foxes and those ugly wolves! Kill them, boys, because their fur is sure going to make a nice coat or two,' cackles Andriana on her broomstick, who looks at Ettore at the back, who is theatrically shaking his paw towards the parachuting animals.

Monica flies up, grabs an incoming parachute from the top, pulls it and the poor bear towards a tree. Fortunately, the bear has the presence to unstrap his parachute and take his chance on landing on the ground. His gamble pays off as he lands with both feet on the head of one of the cyclops, which cushions the Italian bear's fall.

■ ■ ■

'Boris, gather a crew and guard the mothers and children. I am sure the foxes in pyjamas will aid you,' orders Charles.

'It is my duty,' replies Boris.

'Foxham, let's make our stand, for tonight we are the saviours of the world. Are you with me?' shouts Charles.

'We are with you and ready!' shouts George. And with that, all the remaining armed male foxes, humans, dogs and badgers run through the broken steel wall, and downhill towards the battlefield.

Within less than a minute, the sky is filled with the sound of swords and home-made weapons swishing and colliding, with grunts and battle cries.

Leonardo and Francisco land just outside Foxham Hill and waste no time embarking in a melee with two ghouls. The ghouls are powerless to stop the onslaught of these ferocious wolves; their demise is swift but brutal.

Even though the bears of Campania and the foxes from Mario's gang are experienced parachute jumpers, they are having difficulty in landing near the old medieval tower. Some have landed in the village instead, missing the blazing cottages and homes, but still feeling the heat. Some of them have landed in the woods, with the odd fox or bear hanging from a tree, and many have landed on the common, with one fox, Franco, landing in the booby trap in between two spikes, which made poor Franco sweat profusely. Yet these brave and strong animals waste no time in unbuckling their parachutes to join the good fight, be it in the woods or on Foxham Hill.

Enoch is now watching from afar in hiding. However, the dark lord is not shrouded

in fear, as he passionately believes that his army will overcome their opponents with ease and victory will be his.

Enoch's thoughts are broken when he hears a loud grinding engine sound. He turns around to see three red double-decker buses. 'So, it's true what they say in London: wait all day for a bus, then three come at once,' Enoch mutters to himself.

The three red double-decker buses, all missing the booby trap in Foxham High Road, beep their horns in support of the bear and fox parachuters as they pass them on the way to the battlefield.

The buses come to an abrupt halt at the bottom of Foxham Hill, their front and side doors swing open, and out pile a gang of well-dressed black men and smartly dressed foxes; from the third bus, which is packed to the rafters, pour out more well-dressed men and foxes, with Simone Libertazzi, Ferdy, Oliver, Diabolo and 15 Mediterranean-looking men.

'It's my brothers, workmates, neighbours,' declares George as he plunges his sword into a goblin.

'Foxes from East London,' bellows Charles, as he sees off a banshee.

'And my gang,' states a proud Mario, after shooting a ghoul up the backside.

The Notting Hill entourage, the East London foxes with Oliver's brothers Harold and Cropper, led by West Ham Bob, and Mario's men with Simone (who were picked up as they were approaching Foxham, as Diabolo recognised them straight away) rush into the battle with home-made weapons and cricket bats. Ferdy and Oliver do the same, whilst Diabolo straight away knocks out one ghoul, one goblin, one banshee and one cyclops—it is no wonder he is feared in the streets of Naples.

'Oh no! Look at the skies! It's an army of bats,' yells Chester, whilst sword-fighting a banshee, who also stops to see the moonlight sky filled with black flying creatures. Chester sees the banshee drop its guard, takes advantage and now the banshee is no more.

'The vampire came. I knew he would,' chuckles Enoch to himself, at the back of Foxham Wood.

'Chester, they aren't bats, they're crows. It's Gilberto!' yells Betty, who, along with Kaye and Anna, who got punched on the snout by a goblin, have come out of the enclosure of the medieval tower to fight the evil army.

'Oh, xxxx xxxxx xxxxx,' cries out Enoch. (I am sorry I can't repeat these words, as they even offend me.)

Then Enoch gets a moment of inspiration, as one of the buses still has its engine ticking over. Thus, Enoch runs out of Foxham Wood and over to the bus, gets in the driver's seat, puts his foot down on the accelerator, turns the bus around, and spins off. Yet Enoch forgets there is an open booby trap in Foxham's High Road, therefore the bus dives straight into it, with two spikes going past Enoch's right and left ear respectively.

'Mamma,' sobs Enoch, trapped in a double-decker bus in a booby trap.

■ ■ ■

Yes, Gilberto did bump into a fox couple in Norway and the fox was licking his lips, but that was only because the poor fox had chapped lips. Moreover, luckily for Gilberto, the foxes, Mathias and Nora, are the proud parents of Foxham resident Otto.

When Gilberto told them of his conundrum, Mathias summoned a few local crows. Then he asked, with Gilberto acting as the interpreter, for the Norwegian crows to fly with Gilberto to Naples. Once the crows heard about the seriousness of Gilberto's mission, they asked for no reward, as they love the way the world is.

Mathias and Nora were concerned for their son Otto, as when they called his telephone number a few days before bumping into Gilberto, it was out of order and it was the same with other telephone numbers they tried in Foxham. In fact, Mathias was going to send a telegram to Otto that very evening.

Nora, after learning about the plight of the world, ran to a nearby restaurant to use their telephone. She called her sister, Maja, who lives and works in Naples as a chiropodist for foxes in the city. Maja, who has done Silvia's paws on numerous occasions, went into the city to find some of Mario's gang and to inform them of the serious situation in Foxham and that a crow will be arriving shortly.

The moment Gilberto arrived in Naples with his new Norwegian friends, to talk to Mario's gang and their entourage, his Italian crow gang said they wanted to help as they were tired of the witches. The English crows only joined the good fight this morning, when the flock of Italian and Norwegian crows flew pass, saying that they were off to save the world.

So, it was Gilberto eventually getting to Naples that meant Stefano and his friends, the bears of Campania and Mario's gang learnt about the immediate danger that Foxham and the world are in. I promised I would tell you how they found out.

■ ■ ■

As Diabolo was dancing at the Notting Hill social club, with George's brothers Errol and Toby and their friends admiring his suit and moves, Ferdy suddenly remembered the reason why there were in London, and it was not for a jolly up, but to save the world. So, when the inebriated fox told Errol about their mission, within an hour, a tough-yet-loving posse of Notting Hill men residents were ready to rescue the Earth from evil.

Then a merry Oliver recalled they needed to go to Hackney, too, so the Foxham trio could gather a crew of East London foxes for this monumental and dangerous battle. So, they would have to take a detour from West London to East London before setting off to Foxham.

However, the only mode of transport they could source was three red double-decker buses from Errol's yard in Hammersmith where he works as a bus driver.

Just before they left for East London then Norfolk, Errol stated if they bring the buses back in one piece by Easter Monday, then no one will be any the wiser, as Errol had not asked permission to borrow the buses. But unfortunately for Errol, Enoch has already crashed a bus into a booby trap. Yet Errol, smart and a fast talker, is bound to think of something to tell London Buses.

■ ■ ■

'Attack any goblins, ghouls, banshees or cyclops on sight,' orders Gilberto in his cap to his army of crows as they approach the battle of Foxham Hill.

The crows fly down and peck down hard on the foreheads and eyes of any hideous and nasty creature, making them drop their guard and weapons. So, from a bear of Campania to a fox from Hackney, they take full advantage of their opponents' disadvantage.

The witches, Diana and Benedetta, who were knocked off their broomsticks by their own jar spell explosion, are fighting on Foxham Hill; Andriana, with Ettore, Monica and Caterina, are still flying on their broomsticks above the battlefield.

Suddenly, Andriana, with her eagle eyes, notices Trudi, Carlotta and Alberto in the turret of the medieval tower.

Andriana calls to her fellow witches, 'Caterina, use all your exploding jar spells, but keep your distance and don't worry about the casualties of war. Oh, wonderful leader, Monica—fly with me, for there's a fat fox to kill.'

All three witches cackle the traditional cackle, as Andriana with Ettore and Monica flies towards the medieval tower. Caterina flies low down to the ground, weaving in between the odd crow or two. Then the evil witch pulls out two large jars filled with purple and blue smoke from the pockets of her black dress. Caterina drops the jars towards the ground, and says with menace, 'Zacam bang bomb od drix ol foes.'

The moment the glass shatters on the earth, there is a bang louder than thunder and a flash brighter than lightning. The earth and the trees shake, everyone near the explosion is thrown into the air, and the crows are pushed up high and then down to the ground. Even the catalyst herself, Caterina, is not immune to the blast, as she is thrown off her broomstick.

Trudi, Carlotta and Alberto rush to the pinnacle of the tower to see the tragic sight of their fallen army. To make things worse, Carlotta looks up to see a vicious-looking Andriana, with Ettore, and a grotesque-looking Monica flying straight towards them.

All Alberto can say is: 'Oh dear.'

18

The Showdown

Unscathed from the jar spell bomb, the hideous and nasty Diana and Benedetta step out from the trees and into the moonlight. 'Come on, let's slaughter everyone who has landed near the woods,' says a spiteful Diana.

Yet one thing these witches didn't count on or see is Anna Milanese, who is lying only 10 feet away from them, after being thrown into the air by the blast. Anna is not a natural witch like her granddaughter Trudi yet, nevertheless, has enough knowledge and power to stand up to Diana and Benedetta.

As the evil duo walks past the lifeless fox, Anna gains consciousness—perhaps through her intuition—and jumps to her feet. From her overcoat, Anna pulls out clear quartz, looks at the Moon, and nervously chants, 'Graa ol zorge g ol hour c need, please stop ol foes g c blans steps.'

It is a basic restriction spell taught to her by Carlotta that temporarily fixes your opponent on the spot. Empowered by the crystal under the Moon, the success of the spell is only achieved if the witch truly believes in her own power.

Due to lack of experience and participation in battle, Anna's faith is slightly weak. So Benedetta freezes like a statue, yet Diana is unaffected by the spell.

'Silly fox from Milan, you should have spent more time practising magic than cooking. I am going to burn you like a bonfire,' exclaims Diana in a loud and booming voice that awakes both armies.

'That's it, Madame Diana! Show that fox what for!' says a now-awake Goblin, as he gets up from the green grass near the woods.

'Shut up, horrid little thing,' yells Diana, who has never liked the goblins from the onset.

Anna, seeing the disagreement between the Witch from Benevento and a goblin from Norfolk, runs up the hill towards Charles, who too is getting up from the blast. 'Help me, Charles.'

Charles, the brave fox that he is, holds a sword to the air, which he has just found on the ground, and announces, 'Foxham Army, arise and fight!'

Within seconds, George stands up and yells, 'This is it, Foxham! Let's finish the job!'

'I hear you. Come on, crows!' bellows Gilberto.

Now both armies, with some casualties but no fatalities to Foxham, are awake, so battle commences again.

'Oh sxxx, I better flee back to the trees,' says Diana, who punches the goblin who encouraged her in the mouth as she seeks shelter.

Boris, his entourage, the foxes in pyjamas, the mothers and the young folk start to cheer from the tower's enclosure upon seeing Charles, George and Gilberto lead the attack.

■ ■ ■

'Hello, fatty. Remember me?' asks Andriana on her broomstick, with Ettore and Monica by her right-hand side, to Alberto in the turret of the medieval tower.

With pure Napolitano bravery, the fox retorts, 'You should look in the mirror first before you start calling foxes nasty names.'

Ettore chuckles and receives a clip around the ear from Andriana for doing so. Monica, slightly taken aback by what she perceives as insubordination from this jolly young fox, starts to wail like a spoilt brat: 'Fatty, fatty, fatty!'

Alberto, Trudi, and Carlotta start to laugh, thus Monica flies towards the trio, pulls out a spell jar from her satchel, and throws it at them. The glass shatters, which pushes Trudi and Carlotta hard onto the tower's wall, unable to move and speak.

Andriana raises both her arms to the top of her chest, points them towards the tower door and chants, 'Shut od let ag el pass.' The old thick oak door firmly shuts, the large and rusty cast-iron key turns to the right, locking the door in the process, then the key flies directly into the palm of Andriana's right hand, who throws it down to the ground below.

'Oh dear, fatty, your friends can't help you now. In 10 minutes...' (yes, readers, the time has flown and it is nearly midnight) '...we will sacrifice you and that is going to be so much fun,' utters Monica as she and Andriana, on their broomsticks, gently glide down into the turret of the tower. Both, including Ettore, dismount, which makes poor Alberto gulp, as Trudi and Carlotta look on in horror.

Subsequently, Monica pulls out a cold steel jagged dagger from under her cape. The dagger may not look grand by any stretch of the imagination; nevertheless, it looks deadly enough to Alberto, who is quickly forced to the ground by Andriana, with Ettore pinning his shoulders down, making the poor fox unable to move. 'That's it, cat. Hold fatty down for eight more minutes, then I will perform the sacrifice and fulfil our prophecy,' declares Monica.

Suddenly there is a loud bang on the medieval tower door, followed by shouts of, 'Let us in!' It is Boris and his entourage, Silvia, Victoria and a few foxes in pyjamas.

'Be silent, simpletons of Foxham! Soon the world will be ours, and those that survive will be our slaves and tortured every night so you won't be able to sleep,' cackles Monica.

'Never! I will break this door down,' barks courageous Boris.

'Fool! Just listen to this fox scream in pain and beg for his mother,' announces Andriana.

'His mother is here and I swear I will punch you on the nose!' yells Silvia beside Boris, who is trying to kick the door down.

Trudi and Carlotta are trying, through sheer mental strength and focus, to break the spell. Suddenly, Trudi's right paw frees itself from the wall. Ettore, who is facing them as he holds Alberto down, notices the movement from Trudi's paw, so he turns to speak to the witches. Both Trudi and Carlotta hold their breath, believing that their attempt to break the spell is about to be foiled.

'Madame Monica and Madame Andriana, in this new world, will I be donning a new hat every day and eating a fine fish supper every evening?' enquires the black cat in a hat.

'Silence, silly cat! In the new world, you will return to being a normal cat. I will burn all your hats and your meals will be boiled fish heads. For us, the rulers of the new world, we will eat the finest foods, wear the best clothes and live in the grand houses. But servants and fools like you will obey us on your knees for eternity,' says Monica harshly, as she stands over the trembling Alberto, with the dagger in her right hand.

Ettore—who many centuries ago was the familiar for Monica, before becoming the familiar for the next generation of the Witches of Benevento, then Enoch's pet, before converting to his second in command—has always felt he never really belonged to the world of evil. This feeling has been heightened since Ettore discovered he loves wearing an assortment of hats.

Ettore looks directly at Trudi and Carlotta, winks, then returns his attention to Monica, and says the bravest words he has ever spoken. 'Then I, Ettore, do not wish to live in that world. Nor will I let anyone else live in such a cruel and unfair world.'

Monica, in shock from Ettore's bold statement, fails to see the cat leap up onto her chest, who then pushes her to the edge of the medieval tower. 'Get off me, you silly cat!'

But these words are meaningless to Ettore, who musters the energy, force, and commitment to take the final plunge of pushing Monica and himself off the tower and onto the ground.

'No!' screams Andriana, who suddenly feels a punch to her jaw.

It's Carlotta, as she and Trudi have broken free from the spell and the wall. 'Not so tough now, are we, Andriana?' says Carlotta.

Trudi runs over to Alberto. 'It's nearly time. Stay lying down and look at the Moon. I need to rid you of this curse and save the world.'

Alberto, who misses the pizzerias of Naples, playing football in the streets of Naples, and painting Naples on a canvas in his bedroom, doesn't say a word.

Thenceforward, the medieval tower door flies open, but without any force, as Charlie caught the key when Andriana threw it down. But it took the young rascal of a fox awhile to work out what the key was actually for. But once he did, he and his best friend Owen raced to the top of the tower, as they knew Boris and his entourage, Silvia, Victoria and some of the foxes in pyjamas were there.

Silvia pushes Boris out of the way, heads towards Andriana, who is about to fight Carlotta, and without any words punches the witch who, as you remember knows how to box, straight on the nose, as the witch is too slow to guard the punch. Andriana screams out in pain and is then wrestled to the ground by Carlotta, Boris and a few more.

'I told you I would punch you on the nose. Never ever cross a mother from Naples,' declares a proud and strong Silvia.

Then the brave troops from Foxham and the overpowered witch focus their attention on Trudi in silence. Moreover, the only noise they can hear now is the battle of good versus evil on Foxham Hill.

Trudi pulls out from her left dress pocket the bottle of liquid magic from Barbagia and the ancient manuscript that Charles gave her. She rolls out the antique paper from its wooden handles, looks at her new best friend, Carlotta, who is now sitting on top of Andriana, and asks, 'Is it time?'

Carlotta just smiles and nods.

Trudi pours the liquid magic over Alberto's head, who is now past caring, as this adventure has been a lot to take on board. Trudi looks at the Moon, then to her manuscript, and then she pronounces in Latin: 'Carissimi mundi, nos sunt gratus ad pulchritudinem et diliget te da nobis, et ego rogabo unum placet: Ejice hanc adipem vulpes a maledictione auferat ac tenebras et nos lux in sempiternum, et promitto, nullus homo, nullum animal erit lux vos sunt.'

Which roughly translates as: 'Dear world, we are grateful for the beauty and love you give us, and I ask one thing please, rid this kind and happy fox from this curse, take away the darkness and give us light forever. I promise, no human, no animal will let you down.'

As Trudi brings the words that might have just saved the planet to a close, the Moon suddenly brightens up, which is followed by the sound of a rumbling sky. Suddenly, heavy rain falls from the skies onto Foxham. But no one from Foxham is bothered by the downpour, as they have just been fighting the Witches of Benevento, Enoch, goblins, ghouls, banshees and a few cyclops. Therefore, getting wet is certainly not a concern. Then Chester shouts out, 'Look! Our homes are being saved from the fire by the rain!' to which all the good folk of Foxham and their friends cheer loudly.

The rain and thunder come to an abrupt end as the stars start to shine down brightly once again on Foxham.

The goblins, ghouls, banshees and a few cyclops who recovered from the blast slowly start to creep back into the woods, hoping no one will notice, as they now know that they have lost.

Monica is no more—the courageous Ettore saw to that. Andriana is unable to move—not because of Carlotta sitting on her, she is just unable to do so. Diana and Benedetta, after recovering from Anna's spell, are hiding in the woods, yet frozen to the spot on which they stand.

Caterina, who was thrown off her broomstick by the jar spell bomb and was knocked out when she landed, regains consciousness with no idea who she is and why she is in the middle of a skirmish. A scared Caterina tries to get up, but something is holding her down.

All of a sudden, Monica's and the other Witches of Benevento's skin starts to turn a light grey. The witches that are still alive start to scream, yet these screeches are short-lived, as their light-grey skin colour becomes stone, as the witches morph into statues.

One of the goblins in the woods, seeing Diana turn into a hideous statue, cries out, 'Run!'

Diabolo upon hearing the goblin, shouts out, 'Let's get them!'

'No, let them be. We can find them later. We have won, Diabolo,' says Charles.

'Charles is right. It's been a long night. I say we go to the tower for some drinks and food,' adds Mario, who is now standing by Charles.

'Sounds a good idea,' says George, who is also nearby. Then he turns to Thomas, who is standing with Diabolo, and announces, 'Three cheers for Officer Thomas.

Hip hip, hooray!' As they all celebrate, Officer Thomas blushes and from the tower, he can see Charlie and his brother Owen cheering him on. Thomas smiles, knowing they will never tease him again.

Boris and the rest of the entourage start to climb down the stairs of the medieval tower to join the celebrations, after hearing everyone cheering Officer Thomas, leaving Silvia, Trudi, Carlotta, Alberto and a stone statue of Andriana in the turret.

'The mark on your left cheek has gone, Alberto. The curse is well and truly lifted. We won. Well done, Trudi—both of you are brave foxes and Silvia, lovely punch.'

Everyone starts to laugh, then Alberto says with much sadness, 'Ettore really was my friend in the end. He saved us, but not himself.'

All four solemnly walk over to the edge of the tower, look through the curtain wall and onto the ground, where the lifeless body of Ettore lays by the stone statue of Monica.

'I always thought Ettore was on the side of good and he proved it in the end. We will always honour the black cat in a hat who saved the world,' whispers Carlotta to her friends, as she starts to cry.

19

Epilogue

Foxham's Midsummer Gala— Foxham Hill and the Medieval Tower—21st June 1958

'Well, it's true, us cats certainly do have nine lives,' says Ettore, in a brown tweed cheese-cutter hat and taking a bite from a tuna sandwich, to Stefano Romano, his wife Aria, and their two daughters Gabriella and Beatrice, who laugh at the cat's sincere declaration with much love and happiness. For that is the feeling in the air tonight at the Foxham Midsummer Gala—laughter, love and happiness, with much teasing.

So far this evening, Boris has been getting the biggest laugh. As the Calypso band from Notting Hill, close friends of George and Betty, are playing, Boris has decided to get up and dance to this rhythmical, hypnotic and pulsating music. The only problem is Boris cannot dance.

Come on—you didn't expect a summer's evening with a village full of foxes, other animals and humans, the bears of Campania, a gathering from London's West Indian community, foxes from East London, a good witch with an uncanny resemblance to Marilyn Monroe, Mario's posse of tough men and foxes, two boxing wolf brothers and other assortment of wonderful characters to be totally sentimental, did you? No, far from it.

Anyway, Boris doesn't care about the laughter or whether he can dance or not. No one really does, because everyone here is happy to be alive and knowing that the world is safe, for the time being.

Charles Reynard, overwhelmed and delighted by how everyone played a vital part in defeating Enoch and the Witches of Benevento, has made sure that everyone involved, from Rocco, captain of the fishing trawler Viaqua, to Otto's parents Mathias and Nora, is here. Adding to this wonderful array of brave and beautiful souls, there is the ambience and the scenery of Foxham, a great selection of food (West Indian, Italian and British), and a wide variety of beverages, from pop drinks to beer, care of Horace from The Six Bells.

As for the entertainment, comedy and music, after the fantastic Calypso band, Foxham's favourite comedian Basil Brush will take the stage once again, and as the laughter is settling, Foxy and Ferdy will play their favourite rock 'n' roll and jazz records, and the grand finale will be The Quarrymen, back due to popular demand.

When Charles asked George, John and Paul if they wanted to play at Foxham again, they said 'Yes!' without any hesitation. Furthermore, for this evening only, Chester will be playing drums with The Quarrymen, as the Liverpool lads warmed to Chester when they met him earlier this year. Chester is doing the concert just for fun, as he believes he won't make a good living as their drummer.

With more folk than usual for the Foxham Midsummer Gala, all the residents from Oliver to George, have given their spare rooms to guests and Charles has put caravans on Foxham Common, as everyone expects this gala to probably last a week.

■ ■ ■

Ettore, who regained consciousness after pushing Monica off the tower, was ready to leave Foxham that very evening. Even though he was overwhelmed by the applause and praise he received, in fact the cat cried.

However, just as Ettore was about to depart, Charles asked him what job he wanted, other than being a witches' familiar. Ettore rather sheepishly replied, 'To own a hat shop,' to which Charles said, 'See me in a day or two and I will get you that hat shop.'

In just under three months, Ettore's Hats in Foxham has become the hat shop for anyone who is anyone from Norfolk, Cambridgeshire and Essex, with a thriving mail-order business.

Regarding Ferdy, the taxman is still after him. Enough said on that matter for the time being.

■ ■ ■

Foxham, after the damage from the invasion and fire, was rebuilt by the residents. The foxes from East London and George's brothers and friends would come up on their days off to help out, with their travel, labour and board paid for by Charles. And with Foxham Station nearer to completion, the village is bigger and better than before.

Foxham's Italian friends, the Norwegian and London Crows offered to stay on and help to rebuild Foxham, yet Charles thanked them and reassured them it was all covered. But two bears, Beniamino and Guglielmo from the bears of Campania, did stay on and now reside in Foxham. Since helping to rebuild Foxham, they now make hats with Ettore and lodge with the loveable pensioner Reggie.

But this evening, everyone has returned for the Foxham Midsummer Gala.

The Witches of Benevento, now statues, were moved by a crane to the outskirts of Foxham Wood. Now called Witches Corner, it is a popular spot for picnics with the locals as it reminds them of their victory that saved the world.

Yet the world does not know of the courage that took place in Foxham that prevented the dark forces from taking over. For the only mention of the battle of Foxham was a brief article in a newspaper that will remain nameless, stating that five old women were terrorised by Norfolk foxes. Charles believes that Enoch, who fled after crashing the bus and has not been seen since, spoke to his friends, people of influence in the media, hence the brief article. So, the battle will become part of Norfolk's folklore, yet those that know don't care, for they are not after validation and acceptance—they just want to keep the world safe.

At the top of Foxham Hill by the medieval tower stand Trudi and Carlotta with their arms around each other, looking at all the fun and excitement.

'Good to see you again. Are you going to stay on this time?' asks Trudi.

Carlotta looks at her fox friend, smiles and replies, 'Yes, Alberto is now safe, and I just love the Foxes of Foxham.'

■ ■ ■

A dark and damp prison cell, somewhere in Norfolk: 'Would you like your tea and chocolate cake now, Madame Painshill?'

'Yes, Mrs Duke, and be quick about it. I hear that the Witches from Benevento have failed. My great-great-grandmother, June D'abernons, knew Monica well. If my plan of fitting up those nasty cubs had worked, then they—I mean we—would have won. So now we have no choice but to escape.'

'For you see, Mrs Duke, I am a fox witch, with a tie to these witches. Once we get out of here, you will help me to find a manuscript and magic potion in Sardinia that will fulfil a prophecy... The second return of the Witches of Benevento.'

Mrs Duke, who just wanted to serve her prison sentence without any bother, gulps in fear, as Penelope Painshill starts to cackle like the evil witch that she is...

A CRAFTY CIGARETTE
TALES OF A TEENAGE MOD

Foreword by John Cooper Clarke.
'I couldn't put it down because I couldn't put it down.'

'Crafty Cigarette, all things Mod and a dash of anarchy. Want to remember what it was like to be young and angry? Buy this book. A great read.'
Phil Davis (Actor Chalky in Quadrophenia)

'A Great Debut That Deals With The Joys and Pains of Growing Up.'
Irvine Welsh

'A coming of age story, 'A Crafty Cigarette' maybe Matteo Sedazzari's debut novel but it's an impressive story.'
Vive Le Rock

'It's a good book and an easy read. That's pretty much what most pulp fiction needs to be.'
Mod Culture

'A work of genius.'
Alan McGee (Creation Records)

'Like a good Paul Weller concert the novel leaves you wanting more. I'll be very interested in reading whatever Matteo Sedazzari writes next.'
Louder Than War

A mischievous youth prone to naughtiness, he takes to mod like a moth to a flame, which in turn gives him a voice, confidence and a fresh new outlook towards life, his family, his school friends, girls and the world in general. Growing up in Sunbury–on–Thames where he finds life rather dull and hard to make friends, he moves across the river with his family to Walton–on–Thames in 1979, the year of the Mod Revival, where to his delight he finds many other Mods his age and older, and slowly but surely he starts to become accepted...."

A Crafty Cigarette is the powerful story of a teenager coming of age in the 70s as seen through his eyes, who on the cusp of adulthood, discovers a band that is new to him, which leads him into becoming a Mod.

ISBN-13 : 978-1526203564

THE MAGNIFICENT SIX
IN TALES OF AGGRO

Foreword by Drummer Steve White (The Style Council, Paul Weller, Trio Valore,)
'A vivid and enjoyable slice of London life in the 80s, with a wealth of detail and characters,'

'Tales of Aggro has got the feel of 'Green Street' and a touch of 'Lock Stock and Two Smoking Barrels'. This is fiction for realists.'
Vive Le Rock

'A real slice of life told in the vernacular of the streets'
Irvine Welsh

'Laugh out loud funny, exciting and above all, written with real warmth and passion for London and the Character's making their way through this tale and life itself.'
Gents of London

'It's A Treat to Read, Just Like A Crafty Cigarette'
John Cooper Clarke

'Tales of Aggro is lively and funny'
Phil Davis (British Actor - Quadrophenia, Silk, The Firm)

'Tales of Aggro is a kind of time machine that takes one back to the days of 'Scrubbers', 'Scum' and 'Get Carter'. Very redolent of those atmospherics.'
Jonathan Holloway – Theatre Director and Playwright

Meet Oscar De Paul, Eddie the Casual, Dino, Quicksilver, Jamie Joe and Honest Ron, collectively known around the streets of West London as The Magnificent Six. This gang of working-class lovable rogues have claimed Shepherds Bush and White City as their playground and are not going to let anyone spoil the fun.

Meet Stephanie, a wannabe pop star who is determined to knock spots off the Spice Girls, with her girl group. Above all though, meet West London and hear the stories of ordinary people getting up to extraordinary adventures.

Please note that Tales of Aggro is a work of fiction.

ISBN-13 : 978-1527235823

Feltham Made Me – Paolo Sedazzari

Foreword by Mark Savage (Grange Hill)

The poet Richard F. Burton likened the truth to a large mirror, shattered into millions upon millions of pieces. Each of us owns a piece of that mirror, believing our one piece to be the whole truth. But you only get to see the whole truth when we put all the pieces together. This is the concept behind Feltham Made Me. It is the story of three lads growing up together in the suburbs of London, put together from the transcripts of many hours of interview.

ISBN-13 : 978-1527210608

The Secret Life Of The Novel: Faking Your Death is Illegal, Faking Your Life is Celebrated - Dean Cavanagh

"A unique metaphysical noir that reads like a map to the subconscious." **Irvine Welsh**

A militant atheist Scientist working at the CERN laboratory in Switzerland tries to make the flesh into Word whilst a Scotland Yard Detective is sent to Ibiza to investigate a ritual mass murder that never took place. Time is shown to be fragmenting before our very eyes as Unreliable Narrators, Homicidal Wannabe Authors, Metaphysical Tricksters & Lost Souls haunt the near life experiences of an Ampersand who is trying to collect memories to finish a novel nobody will ever read. Goat Killers, Apocalyptic Pirate Radio DJ's, Dead Pop Stars, Social Engineers and Cartoon Characters populate a twilight landscape that may or may not exist depending on who's narrating at the time.

ISBN-13 : 978-1527201538

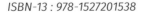

7P'S Paperback – A.G.R

The 7 P's. An unusual title you may think, but its meaning will become as apparent to you as it did for four friends and comrades who, in a desperate move of self-preservation, escaped the troubles of 1980s Northern Ireland, and their hometown of Belfast, only to find themselves just as deep, if not deeper, in trouble of a different kind on the treacherous streets of London.

ISBN-13 : 978-1527258365

ZANI ON SOCIAL MEDIA

After enjoying *Tales from The Foxes of Foxham*, please follow ZANI on Social Media.

ZANI is a passionate and quirky entertaining online magazine covering contemporary, counter and popular culture.

Follow ZANI on Twitter
twitter.com/ZANIEzine

Follow ZANI on FaceBook
www.facebook.com/zanionline?fref=ts

Follow ZANI on Instagram
www.instagram.com/zanionline/